I0610226

José M. de Alencar

Iraçéma - The Honey-Lips

a legend of Brazil

José M. de Alencar

Iraçéma - The Honey-Lips
a legend of Brazil

ISBN/EAN: 9783337389956

Printed in Europe, USA, Canada, Australia, Japan

Cover: Foto ©Andreas Hilbeck / pixelio.de

More available books at **www.hansebooks.com**

IRAÇÉMA

THE HONEY-LIPS

A LEGEND OF BRAZIL

BY

J. DE ALENCAR

TRANSLATED, WITH THE AUTHOR'S PERMISSION,

BY

ISABEL BURTON

LONDON
BICKERS & SON, 1 LEICESTER SQUARE
1886

PREFACE.

I CANNOT allow my readers to remain ignorant of the name of Senhor J. de Alencar, the author of this and several other works; for he deserves to be as well known in England as in Brazil, and it must be the result of the usual modesty of a really clever man that he is not so.

He is their first prose and romance writer. His style, written in the best Portuguese of the present day—one to be learnt and copied—is in thorough good taste and feeling. It contains poetic and delicate touches, and beauty in similes, yet it is real and true to life.

I cannot thank him sufficiently for having allowed so incompetent a translator as myself to be the first to introduce him to the British public. I have endeavoured to be as literal as possible, but I cannot pretend to do him justice, for our harsh Northern tongue only tells coarsely a tale full of grace and music in the Portuguese language; but I have done my best, and if he permits me to translate all his works, I hope to do better as I go on, especially if he will again—as he has already done —give me instructions in Tupy, the language of the aborigines.

ISABEL BURTON.

Santos São Paulo, Brazil.

HISTORICAL ARGUMENT.

—▸◂—

This legend of the aborigines is laid in Ceará, a northern province of Brazil, at that time unknown and unconquered.

In 1603, Pero Coelho, a gentleman of Parahyba, another northerly province, then already belonging to the Portuguese, arrived at the mouth of the river Jaguaribe in Ceará, with a command of 80 colonists and 800 Indians. He there founded the first settlement in Ceará, and called it Nova Lisboa.

This Pero Coelho was abandoned by his comrades when a certain João Soromenho was sent to him with reinforcements, and was authorised to pay the expenses of the expedition by making captives or slaves. He did not respect even the Indians of the Jaguaribe river, who were friendly to the Portuguese.

This proved the downfall of the growing settlement. The natives resented such tyranny. Pero Coelho, with his wife and young children, was compelled to fly by land to his own province.

In the first expedition was Martim Soares Moreno, a youth from Rio Grande do Norte, another northerly province belonging to the Portuguese. He entered into bonds of friendship with Jacaúna and his brother Poty, who were chiefs of the Indians of the seaboard. In 1608, by order of Dom Diogo Menezes, he returned to establish a colony, and in 1611 he founded the fortified place of Nossa Senhora do Amparo, or " Our Lady of Protection."

Jacaúna, who lived on the borders of Acáracú— " River of the Heron's nest "—settled near it with his tribe, to protect it from the Indians of the interior, and from the French, who then infested the coast.

Poty eventually became a Christian, and was baptized Antonio Phelipe Camarão. He highly distinguished himself when the Dutch invaded the coast, and his services were richly rewarded by the Portuguese Government.

Martim Soares Moreno became a Field-Marshal, and was one of those brave Portuguese leaders who delivered Brazil from the Hollander invasion. Ceará should honour his memory as that of a good and valiant man, and—the first settlement by Coelho at the mouth of the Jaguaribe having proved a failure— hold him to be her true founder.

My readers will better understand this tale by my explaining that the Pytiguáras were an aboriginal tribe who occupied the shores between Parnahyba and the Jaguaribe, or Rio Grande.

Their chiefs were Jacaúna and Poty (afterwards Camarão, "the Prawn "), two brothers, who were firm allies to the Portuguese. They were at war with the Tabajáras, another tribe occupying the mountains of

Ibyapaba, and the interior as far as the province of Piauhy.

The Chiefs of these inland people were also two. The first was Irapúam, which, translated into Portuguese, means Mel Redondo, or " Round Honey," a wild and vicious bee of that name. This famous bloodthirsty chief ruled in Ceará, but Gráo Deabo— Big Devil—was Lord of the Tabajáras in Piauhy. Both were bitter enemies of the Portuguese, and allied themselves with the French of Maranhão—another northerly province—who had penetrated into and taken possession of the lands as far as the mountain range of Ibyapaba.

IRAÇÉMA.

CHAPTER I.

WILD green seas of my Native Land, where sings the
Jandáia-bird [1] in the fronds of the Carnaúba-palm ! [2]

Green seas which sparkle like liquid emerald in the
rays of the orient sun, as ye stretch along the snowy
beaches shaded by the cocoa-tree !

Be still, ye green seas ! and gently smooth the impetuous wave, that yon venturesome barque may softly
glide over thy waters.

Where goes that hardy Jangada-raft,[3] which rapidly
flies from the Ceará coast, with her broad sail spread
to the fresh breeze of land ?

Where goes it, like the white halcyon seeking his
native rock in the ocean solitudes ?

Three beings breathe upon that fragile plank, which
scuds so swiftly out—far into the open sea.

A warrior youth, whose pale skin betokens that the
blood of the Indians does not colour his veins ; a

---

[1] *Jandáia* is a small yellow, red, and green talking parroquet.

[2] *Carnaúba*, a well-known Brazilian palm of large size, with
many thorny branches all the way up the trunk, instead of being
plain and smooth. Each branch-tip is like a fan-palm. When
young, it has a large fruit, full of oil, which is given to pigs and
cattle. When grown up, its fan-leaves, dried, thatch the houses,
and make hats and mats ; its thorny branches are used for stakes ;
it also has a delicious small black fruit, and from other parts they
extract wax for making the Carnaúba candles.

[3] *Jangada*, a raft.

child, and a mastiff, who both first saw the light in the cradle of the forest, and who sport like brothers, the sons of the same savage soil.

The intermittent breathings from the shore waft an echo which, rising high above the ripple of the waves, sounds forth—

"Iraçéma!" * * *

The young warrior, leaning against the mast, raises his eyes, which are fixed upon the fleeting outline of the shadowy shore. From time to time his sight becomes dim, and a tear falls upon the Giráo-bench,[1] where frolic the two innocents, the companions of his misfortune.

At such moments his soul flies to his lips in a bitter smile.

What left he in that land of exile?

A tale which they told me on the beautiful plains that saw my birth, during the hush of night, whilst the moon, sailing through the heavens, silvered the prairies; whilst the breezes murmured amid the palm groves.

The wind freshens.

The surf rolls in higher billows. The barque leaps upon the waves—disappears on the horizon. Wide yawns the waste of waters. The storm broods, condor-like, with dusky wings over the abyss.

God keep thee safe, stout barque, amidst the boiling billows! God steer thee to some friendly bight! May softer breezes waft thee, and for thee may the calm jasper seas be like plains of milk!

But whilst thou sailest thus at the mercy of the winds, graceful barque, waft back to that white beach some of the yearning[2] that accompanies thee, but which may not leave the land to which it returns.

---

[1] *Giráo*, a sort of rude bench for sitting upon in the Jangada raft.

[2] Yearning, in the original *saudade*—an untranslatable Portuguese word for which we have no equivalent; it means a soft sad regret for some person, place, or happy time missed and past—in fac', the Latin *desiderium*.

CHAPTER II.

FAR, very far from that Serra which purples the horizon, was born Iraçéma.

Iraçéma, the virgin with the honey lips,[1] whose hair, hanging below her palm-like[2] waist, was jetty as the Graúna[3] bird's wing.

The comb of the Játy-bee[4] was less sweet than her smile, and her breath excelled the perfume exhaled by the vanilla[5] of the woods.

Fleeter than the wild roe, the dark virgin wandered freely through the plains and forests of Ipú,[6] where her warlike tribe, a part of the great Tabajára[7] nation, lay wigwamed. Her subtle, naked foot scarcely pressed to earth the thin green garment with which the early rains clothe the ground.

One day, when the sun was in mid-day height, she was reposing in a forest-clearing. The shade of the Oitycíca,[8] more refreshing than the dew of night, bathed her form. The arms of the wild acacia dropped their blossoms upon her wet hair. The birds hidden in the foliage sang for her their sweetest songs.

Iraçéma left the bath. Pearl drops of water stood upon her, like the sweet Mangába,[9] which blushes in

---

[1] *Iraçéma* literally means " Lips of Honey."

[2] The Indians, speaking of a tall straight graceful figure, generally use the palm-tree as a simile.

[3] *Graúna* is a bird known by its shining black plumage and sweet song.

[4] *Játy* is a little bee which makes delicious honey.

[5] The vanilla tree, *Baunilha.*

[6] *Ipú*, a district in Ceará, in which there were spots of wonderfully fertile land.

[7] *Tabajára* literally means " Lord of the Villages."

[8] *Oitycíca*, a leafy tree whose shade exhales a delicious freshness.

[9] *Mangába*, the fruit of the Mangábeira, the milk of which tree resembles indiarubber.

the refreshing dawn-dew. Whilst reposing she refits her arrows with the plumes of the Gará,[1] whilst she joins in the joyous song of the forest Sabiá,[2] perched in the nearest bough.

A beautiful Ará,[3] her companion and friend, plays near her. Now the bird climbs the branches and calls the virgin by her name; then he slips down and shakes the little satchel[4] of coloured straw in which the wild maid carries her perfumes, her white threads of the Crautá,[5] her needles of Jussára-thorn,[6] with which she works the grass-cloth, and her dyes that serve to tinge the cotton.

A suspicious noise breaks the soft harmony of the siesta. Iraçéma raises the eyes which no sun can dazzle, and her sight is troubled.

Standing before her, absorbed in gazing upon her, is a strange warrior, if indeed it *is* a warrior, and not some evil spirit of the forest.[7] His face is white as the sands that border the sea, his eyes are sadly blue as the deep. He bears unknown weapons, and is clad in unknown cloths.

Rapid as her eye-glance was the action of Iraçéma. An arrow shot from the bow, and red drops ran down the face of the unknown.

---

[1] *Gará* or *Guará*, the ibis of Brazil, a bird of the marshes, with beautiful red colour.

[2] *Sabiá*, a well-known bird about the size of our thrush, which sings beautifully, and can be taught like a bullfinch. It is the nightingale, the bulbul of South America.

[3] *Ará*, parroquet.

[4] *Urú*. I have called it satchel, but it is a little coffer or basket, in which the savages keep their treasures, and which accompanies them as does a lady's dressing-case in Europe.

[5] *Crautá*, a bromelia or wild pine-apple, from which are drawn fibres finer than thread.

[6] *Jussára*, a palm with large thorns, which are used here even in these days to divide the threads in making lace.

[7] *Máo espirito da floresta*. The natives called those evil spirits *Caa-pora*, "an invisible misfortune." Those who lived in the forest were most feared.

At the first impulse his nimble hand sought his sword-cross; but presently he smiled.

The young warrior had been brought up in the religion of his mother, wherein Woman is a symbol of tenderness and love. He suffered more in his soul than from his wound.

What expression was in his eye and whole face—who knows? But it made the virgin cast away her bow and Uiraçába,[1] and run to the warrior, pained at the pain she had caused. The hand so swift to strike more rapidly and gently staunched the dripping stream.

Then Iraçéma brake the murderous arrow. She offered the shaft to the unknown, and she kept the barbed point.

The warrior spoke:—

" Dost thou break with me the arrow of peace? "[2]

" Who taught the white warrior the tongue of Iraçéma's brethren? How came he to these forests, which never saw other warrior like to him? "

" Daughter of the forests, I come from afar: I come from the land which thy brothers once possessed, and wherein mine now dwell."

" Welcome be the stranger to the Prairie of the Tabajáras, Lords of the Villages, and to the wigwam of Araken, father of Iraçéma."

CHAPTER III.

THE stranger followed the virgin through the glades.

When the last sun-rays fell upon the crest of the

---

[1] *Uiraçába* (aljava), quiver for arrows.

[2] *Guebrar a frecha.* To break an arrow with an Indian was a bond of alliance which could not be broken. It was owing to this circumstance, and to Martim Soares Moreno throwing away his European costume, and dressing and painting like the Red Men, entering also into their customs and language, that he acquired such an influence over them.

mountains, and the turtle-dove cooed forth her first
lament from the forest depths, they sighted upon the
plain beneath them the great Taba ; [1] farther on,
hanging as it were from a rock, under the shade of
the lofty Joaseiro,[2] the wigwam of the Pagé.[3]

The ancient man was seated at the doorway upon
a mat of Carnaúba, smoking and meditating on the
sacred rites of Tupan.[4]   The gentle breath of the
breeze fluttered his hair — long, thin, and white
as flocks of wool. So statue-like was he, that life
only appeared in his hollow, sunken eyes and deep
wrinkles.

The Pagé descried, nevertheless, from afar the two
forms, advancing, he thought, towards a solitary tree,
whose dense foliage was casting a long shadow adown
the valley before him.

When the travellers entered the deep gloom of the
wood, his eye, made, like the tiger's, for darkness,
recognised Iraçéma, and saw that she was followed
by a young warrior of a strange race and a far-off
land.

The Tabajára [5] tribes beyond Ibyapába were full
of a new race of warriors, pale as the flowers of the
storm,[6] and coming from the remotest shores to the
banks of the Mearim.[7]   The old man thought that it
was one of these warriors who trod his native ground.

Calmly he awaited.

---

[1] *Taba*, a village settlement.
[2] *Joaseiro*, a tree which produces the *joaz* fruit, the jujube.
[3] *Pagé*, priest, Druid, magician, soothsayer, or fetish-man.
[4] *Tupan*, the Great Spirit—Thunder, and, since their con-
version, the Consecrated Host of the Tupy Indians.
[5] *Ibyapaba*, the Serra or mountain range which bounds the
province of Ceará, and separates it from Piauhy.
[6] In the original, *alvos como flores de borrasca*. They speak of
white clouds announcing a storm, and this is, literally, "white
as the flowers of the storm."
[7] *Mearim*, a river which rises in Maranhão, and empties
itself into the ocean.

The virgin advancing, pointed to the stranger and said :—

" He came, father."

" He came well. Tupan sent this guest to the wigwam of Araken."

And thus saying the Pagé passed the calumet [1] to the stranger, and they both entered the wigwam.

The youth took the principal hammock, which was suspended in the centre of the habitation. Iraçéma lighted the fire of hospitality, and brought out food to satisfy hunger and thirst. She produced the spoils of the chase, farinha-water, wild-fruits, honeycombs, wine of the Cajú [2] and the pine-apple.

The virgin then went to the nearest spring of fresh water, and returned with the full Igaçába,[3] to wash the stranger's hands and face. When the warrior had eaten, the venerable Pagé extinguished the Caximbo and spoke for the first time.

" Thou camest ? " [4]

" I came," replied the unknown.

" Thou camest well. The stranger is master in the wigwam of Araken. The Tabájaras have a thousand warriors to defend him, and women without number to serve him. Let him speak, and all will obey him."

"Pagé ! I thank thee for thy hospitality. As soon as the sun shall be born, I leave thy wigwam and thy

[1] Calumet, original *caximbo*, the pipe of hospitality.

[2] *Cajú*, the cashew of India—a tree with a fruit like an apple : it is singular because, unlike other fruit, its nut is outside at the top, as if a schoolboy had stuck it in for fun. This must not be confounded with the *Cajá*, which is another Brazilian fruit like a yellow plum.

[3] *Igaçába*, a large earthen pot or jar for wine or any other liquor.

[4] *Vieste* (?) *Vim.* The salutation of hospitality was—

Tupy.	*Brazilian.*	*English.*
Ere wubê.	Tu vieste.	Thou camest.
l'a-aiotu.	Vim, sim.	I came, yes.
Auge-be.	Bemdito.	Be blessed.

prairies, where I strayed, but I would not leave them
without telling thee who the warrior is whom thou
hast made thy friend."

"It is Tupan whom the Pagé serves. He sent him
a guest, and he will take him away again. Araken
has as yet done nothing for him. He does not ask
whence he comes nor whither he goes. If he would
sleep, may the happy dreams descend upon him ; if
he would speak, Araken listens."

The stranger said :—

"I am of the white warriors who raised a Taba on
the banks of the Jaguaribe,[1] near the sea, where dwell
the Pytiguáras,[2] who hate thy blood. My name is
Martim,[3] which in thy tongue means Son of a Warrior.
My race is that of the Great People who first saw the
lands of thy country.[4] Even now my brethren, routed
and beaten back, return by sea to the margins of the
Parahyba,[5] whence they came, and my chief,[6] abandoned by all, crosses the vast regions of the Apody.[7]
Of so many I alone remain, because I was amongst
the Pytiguáras of the Acaraú,[8] in the wigwam of the
valiant Poty, brother of Jacaúna, who planted with
me the Friendship-tree. Three suns have set since
we went forth on the hunting path. I lost sight of

---

[1] *Jaguaribe*, the largest river of the province of Ceará : from
jaguar, small tiger, and *ibe*, plenty.

[2] *Pytiguáras*, the great Indian nation who inhabited the lit-
toral of the province from Parahyba to Rio Grande do Norte,
whose chiefs were Poty and Jacaúna, brothers, and firm friends
of Martim Soares Moreno, and of all the Portuguese. They
were at war with the Tabajáras and the French.

[3] Descendant of Mars.

[4] The Portuguese.

[5] *Parahyba*, a province south-east of Ceará on the Atlantic.

[6] *Pero Coelho* and his party.

[7] The *Sertão desconhecido* or unknown regions of Rio Grande
do Norte, the most north-easterly province of Brazil on the
Atlantic.

[8] *Acaraú*, or "Stream of the Herons," also called *Acáracú*,
"Stream of the Herons' Nests," a river of Ceará.

my friends, and thus I strayed to the prairies of the Tabajáras."

"It was some bad spirit of the forest that blinded the pale-face warrior in the darkness of the woods," replied the old man.

The Cauâm [1] chirped at the other end of the valley. Night had set in.

CHAPTER IV.

THE Pagé shook the Maraca-rattle [2] and left the cabin, but the stranger remained not alone.

Iraçéma returned with the maidens summoned to serve the guest of Araken and the warriors who came to obey him.

" May happiness rock the White Warrior's hammock during the night, and may the sun bring light to his eyes and joy to his soul."

Thus saying, Iraçéma's lip trembled, and the tear stood in her eye.

"Thou leavest me then?" asked Martim.

"The most beautiful virgins [3] of the great Taba remain with the warrior."

"The daughter of Araken was mistaken in bringing them here for the guest of the Pagé."

"Iraçéma may not wait upon the stranger. It is she who guards the secret of the Juréma [4] and the

---

[1] *Cauâm*, a bird of evil omen, which feeds on serpents, and chirps its own name.

[2] *Maracá*, an instrument used in the religious and war-like ceremonies of the Indians ; a kind of loud rattle.

[3] *As mais bellas mulheres.* Any Indian's idea of complete hospitality.

[4] *Juréma*, a kind of acacia with thick foliage. It has a bitter fruit and acrid smell, and, mixed with the pulp of its own leaves and other ingredients, it made a kind of hasheesh, which is said to have produced vivid and happy dreams. The making of this dram was kept secret by the Pagés.

mystery of dreams.　Her hand prepares for the Pagé the drink of Tupan."

The Christian warrior crossed the wigwam and disappeared in the darkness.

The great village lay in the bottom of the valley, which was illuminated by bonfires.　Loud rattled the Maracá.　The savages were dancing and beating time to their slow surging of the savage song.　The inspired Pagé headed the sacred rejoicing, and taught to the believers the secrets of Tupan.　The principal chief of the Tabajára nation, Irapúam,[1] had descended from the highest point of the Ibyapaba Serra, to lead the inland tribes against the Pytiguára foe.　The warriors of the valley celebrate the arrival of the chief and the coming fight.

The Christian youth saw from afar the glare of the feast-fire, and walked on, gazing at the deep-blue, cloudless sky.　The " Dead Star "[2] glittered upon the dome of the forest, and guided his firm step towards the fresh banks of the Acaraú.

When he crossed the valley, as if about to enter the forest, the figure of Iraçéma arose before him.　The virgin had followed the stranger like the soft and subtle breeze which passes through the tangled wood without stirring a leaf.

"Wherefore," she murmured, "has the stranger left the Wigwam of Hospitality without taking with him the Gift of Return?[3]　Who harmed the pale-faced warrior in the land of the Tabajáras?"

---

[1] *Irapúam* was the celebrated Tabajára chief in Ceará.　The word means *Mel-Redondo* in Portuguese, in English Round-Honey.　He was so called after a wild and vicious bee of that name, whose honeycomb is round.　Irapúam was a bloodthirsty chief, and his tribe were bitter enemies of the Pytigúaras, and their allies the Portuguese.　They supported the French of Maranhão.

[2] *Estrella morta*, dead star.　They so called the Polar star on account of its immobility, and it was their guide by night.

[3] *O presente da volta*, a hospitable Indian custom.

The Christian felt the justice of her complaint and his own ingratitude.

"Daughter of Araken! No one hurt thy guest. It was a longing to see his friends which made him leave the prairies of the Tabajáras. He did not take the Return Gift, but he carries in his heart the memory of Iraçéma."

"If the memory of Iraçéma dwelt in the heart of the stranger, it would not suffer him to depart. The wind blows not away the sand of the desert when the sand has drank deep of the water of rain."

And the virgin sighed.

"The pale-faced warrior should wait till Cauby returns from hunting. The brother of Iraçéma has quick ears. He can hear the Boicininga [1] amidst all the noises of the forest. He has the eyes of the Oitibó, [2] which sees best in the dark. Cauby will guide him to the banks of the river of the herons."

"How long will it be before the brother of Iraçéma returns to the wigwam of Araken?"

"The rising sun will bring the warrior Cauby to the plains of the Ipú."

"Thy guest will wait, daughter of Araken; but if the returning sun bring not the brother of Iraçéma, it will take the pale-faced warrior to the Taba of the Pytiguáras."

And Martim returned to the cabin of the Pagé. The white hammock, perfumed by Iraçéma with Beijoim, [3] gave the guest a calm and sweet sleep. The Christian was lullabied to sleep by the murmurs of the forest and the low tender song of the Indian maid.

---

[1] *Boicininga*, rattlesnake.

[2] *Oitibó*, a night-bird of the owl family.

[3] *Benzoin*, in the original *Beijoim* or *Beijuim*, an odoriferous drug.

CHAPTER V.

THE Prairie-cock raises his scarlet crest from out his home. His clear trill announces the approach of day.

Darkness still covers the earth, but already the savage people roll up the hammocks in the great Taba, and walk towards the bath. The old Pagé, who had watched all night, talking to the stars, and conjuring the bad spirits of the darkness,[1] entered furtively into the wigwam.

Lo! thundered forth the Boré,[2] filling the valley with its booming sound.

The active warriors seize their weapons and rush to the prairies; when all were collected in the large and circular Ocára,[3] the chief Irapúam sounded the war-cry.

"Tupan gave to the great Tabajára nation all these grounds. We guard the Serras which supply with water the rivers and the fresh Ipús,[4] where grows the maníva,[5] and the cotton. We have abandoned to the barbarous Potyuára,[6] Eaters of Prawns, the naked sands of the sea, with the table-lands wanting wood and water. Now these fishers of the beach, always conquered, give sea-way to the white race, the Warriors

[1] *Os máos espiritos da treva :* the savages call these spirits *Curupira*, wicked imps.

[2] *Boré* or *Muré* means a pipe of bamboo, which gives out a hollow, roaring sound.

[3] *Ocára*, a circular space in the centre of a village, upon which all the wigwams open.

[4] *Ipú*, a small fertile oasis in the prairies.

[5] *Maníva* is the root of mandioca, which is like our parsnip, but larger. The Indians dry and grind it, make bread of it, or eat it as farinha (flour).

[6] *Potyuára* means a "*Comedor de Camarão*," or "Eater of the Prawn." This was a spiteful soubriquet given to the Pytiguáras by their enemies, because they lived on the shores and chiefly ate fish.

of Fire,[1] the enemies of Tupan. Already the Emboabas[2] have stood upon the Jaguaribe river. Soon they will be in the prairies of the Tabajáras, and with them the Potyuáras. Shall we—Lords of the Villages —do like the dove, who hides in her nest while the serpent curls himself along the branches?"

The excited chief brandishes his tomahawk,[3] and hurls it into the middle of the circle. Bending down his forehead, he hid his eyes, ruddy with rage. "Irapúam has spoken," at length he said.

The youngest of the warriors advances.

"The Sparrow-hawk hovers in the air. When the Nhambú[4] rises, he falls from the clouds and tears out his victim's heart. The young Tabajára warrior, son of the Serra, is like the sparrow-hawk."

The Poçema[5] of war thunders and re-echoes. The young warrior lifted up the tomahawk, and in his turn brandished it. Whirled rapidly and menacingly in the air, the chief's weapon passed from hand to hand.

The venerable Andíra, brother of the Pagé, let it fall, and stamped upon the ground with his foot, still firm and active.

The Tabajáras are struck by this unusual action. A vote of peace from such a tried and impetuous warrior! The old hero, who grew to bloodshed as he grew in years—the ferocious Andíra—is it he who lets fall the tomahawk, herald of the coming struggle?

Uncertain and silent, all gave ear.

"Andíra, the old Andíra, has drank more blood in

[1] *Guerreiros de fogo,* "warriors of fire," the Portuguese.

[2] *Emboabos,* a name given to the Portuguese, and afterwards to all strangers, on account of their trousers. Its literal meaning is a fowl with feathers down its legs, and alludes to the European practice of wearing nether garments.

[3] *Tacapé,* tomahawk.

[4] *Nhambú,* the Brazilian partridge.

[5] *Poçema,* the great noise made by the savages on solemn occasions—war or triumph. It consisted of clapping their hands and beating palms, accompanied by war-cries or shouts.

war than all these warriors who now gladden the light
of his eyes have drank Cauim [1] at the feasts of Tupan.
He has seen more combats in his life than moons
which have stripped his brow. How many Potynára
skulls has his implacable hand scalped before Time
plucked off his first hair! And old Andíra never
feared that the enemy would tread his native
ground; he rejoiced at their coming, and, as the
breath of winter revives the dried tree, he felt youth
return to his decrepid body when he scented the war
from afar. The Tabajáras are prudent. They will
lay aside the Tomahawk to play the Memby [2] at the
feast. Let Irapúam celebrate the coming of the
Emboábas, and give them all time to swarm upon our
plains. Then Andíra promises him the banquet of
victory."

Irapúam could no longer restrain his fury.

"The Old Bat [3] can remain hidden amongst the
wine-jars, because he fears the light of day, because
he drinks the blood only of the sleeping victim.
Irapúam carries the war at the point of his tomahawk. The terror which he inspires flies forward with
the hoarse boom of the Boré. The Potyuára already
trembles as he hears it roaring in the Serra, roaring
louder than the rebounding of the sea."

CHAPTER VI.

MARTIM strolls pace by pace amongst the tall Joazeiros which encircle the wigwam of the Pagé.

---

[1] *Cauim*, wine of the Cajú.
[2] *Memby*, horn or trumpet.
[3] *Andíra* means "Velho Morcego," or "Old Bat;" hence
the taunt of Irapúam.

It was the hour in which the sweet Aracaty [1] comes up from the sea and spreads over the arid plains its delicious freshness. The plant breathes, and a gentle shiver upraises the green tresses of the forest.

The Christian looks upon the setting sun. The shadow gliding down the mountains and covering the valley enters into his soul. He thinks of his native place and the beloved ones he has left behind. He wonders if he shall some day see them again. Nature all round bewails the death of day. Murmurs the tremulous, tearful wave ; moans the breeze in the foliage ; even silence is sorrowful.

Iraçéma stood before the young warrior.

" Is it the presence of Iraçéma that disturbs the peace of the stranger's brow ? "

Martim looked softly in the virgin's face.

" No, daughter of Araken ! thy presence gladdens me like the morning light. It was the memory of my native land that brought a saudade to my anxious soul."

" A bride awaits him there ? "

The stranger averted his eyes. Iraçéma's head sank upon her shoulder, like the tender palm of the Carnaúba when the rain overhangs the plains.

" She is not sweeter than Iraçéma, the maiden of the honied lips, nor more beautiful ! " murmured the guest.

" The forest flower is beautiful when it has a branch to shelter it, a trunk round which to entwine itself. Iraçéma does not live in the soul of a warrior. She never felt the freshness of his smile."

Silent were both ; their eyes fell to the ground. They heard nought save the beating of their hearts.

---

[1] *Aracaty*, the savages of the interior so call the sea-breezes, which blow regularly towards the evening over the valley of the Jaguaribe, and refresh the interior after the scorching heat of summer days. Aracaty is the quarter whence comes the monsoon, and in some Brazilian places the evening sea-breeze still retains that name.

The virgin was the first to speak.

"Gladness shall soon return to the heart of the pale-faced warrior, because Iraçéma wishes that before nightfall he may see the bride who expects him."

Martim smiled at the young girl's artless wish.

"Come!" said the virgin.

They crossed the forest and descended into the valley. The wood was thick on the hill-skirts; a dense dome of dark-green foliage protected the sylvan shrine dedicated to the mysteries of barbarous rites.

This was the sacred wood of the Juréma. Around stood the rugged trunks of the Tupan tree; from the boughs, hidden by thick greenery, hung the sacrificial vases; ashes of the extinct fire, which had been used for the feast of the last new moon, still strewed the ground.

Before entering this place of mystery, the virgin, who was leading the warrior by the hand, hesitated, and applied her subtle ear to the sighings of the breeze. Each slight noise of the forest had a meaning for the wild daughter of the desert. However, there was nothing suspicious in the deep respiration of the forest.

Iraçéma signed to the stranger to wait and be silent, whilst she disappeared in the thickest of the wood. The sun still hung over the mountain ridge, and night began to shroud the solitary spot.

When the virgin returned, she brought in a leaf some drops of an unknown green liquor, poured from an Igaçába, which she had taken out of the ground. She presented the rude bowl to the warrior.

"Drink!"

Martim felt a sleep like death take possession of his eyes; but soon his soul seemed full of light, and strength exhilarated his heart. He lived over again days better and happier than any that he had ever known. He enjoyed the reality of his brightest hopes.

Behold! he returns to his native land. He kisses his aged mother. He sees the pure angel of his boyish love, more beautiful and more tender than before.

Then why, hardly returned to his native home, does the young warrior again abandon his father's roof and seek the desert?

Now he crosses the forests; now he arrives at the plains of the Ipú. He seeks in the forest the daughter of the Pagé. He follows the slight trail of the coy virgin, incessantly sighing forth her sweet name to the breeze :—

"Iraçéma! Iraçéma!" . . .

Now he finds her, and winds his arm round her sweet form.

The young girl, yielding to the warm pressure, hides her face upon the warrior's bosom, and trembles there like a timid partridge when its tender mate ruffles with the beak its delicate plume.

The warrior more than once sighed forth her name, and sobbed as though to summon another loving lip. Iraçéma felt her soul escaping to merge itself in a fiery kiss.

And his brow bent low, and already the flower of her smile hung down as though calling to be culled.

Suddenly the virgin trembled. Quickly disengaging herself from the arm that encircled her, she seized her bow.

CHAPTER VII.

IRAÇÉMA threaded the trees silent as a shade; her sparkling eyes pierced through the foliage like starbeams. She listened to the profound silence of the night and inhaled the balm-blowing breeze.

She stopped. A shadow glided amongst the

B

boughs and the leaves were crackled by a light step,
unless indeed the report was the buzzing of some
insect. Slowly the soft sound waxed louder, and with
it the shadow became darker.

It was a warrior.

With one bound the virgin confronted him, trembling with fear, and still more with wrath.

"Iraçéma!" exclaimed the brave, recoiling.

"The Anhánga[1] hath doubtless disturbed the sleep
of Irapúam, that he has lost himself in the Juréma
wood, where no warrior enters save by the will of
Araken."

"It was not the Anhánga, but the thought of
Iraçéma that disturbed the sleep of the bravest of
the Tabajára braves. Irapúam hath descended from
his eyrie to follow up the plain the white crane of the .
river. He came, and Iraçéma fled from his gaze.
The voices of the Taba related in the hearing of the
Chief that a stranger had sat under the roof-tree of
Araken."

The virgin trembled. The warrior fixed upon her
his burning eyes.

The heart here in Irapúam's breast became a tiger's
heart. It panted with rage. He came scenting the
quarry.

"The stranger is in this wood, and Iraçéma accompanied him. Irapúam will drink all his blood :
when that of the white warrior shall fill the veins of
the Tabajára Chief, perhaps the daughter of Araken
may love him."

The maiden's black pupils flashed in the dark, and
a smile of contempt dropped from her lips, bitter as
the gouts of caustic milk which the Euphorbia sheds.

"Never will Iraçéma give herself to the basest of
the Tabajára braves. The spirit of Tupan alone fills

---

[1] *Anhánga,* the spirit of evil. A ghost is also thus called,
the word being composed of *anho,* alone, and *anga,* a soul or
spirit. Thus it means a spirit simply, a phantom.

her breast. Vile is the vampire that hides from the light and drinks the blood of the sleeping victim."

" Daughter of Araken ! provoke not the Ounce. The name of Irapúam flies farther than the Goaná[1] of the lake when he scents the rain beyond the mountains. Let the white warrior appear, and let Iraçéma open her arms to the victor."

" The white warrior is the guest of Araken. Peace brought him to the plains of Ipú, and peace guards him here. Whoso offends the stranger shall offend the Pagé."

The Tabajára chief roared lion-like in his rage.

"The fury of Irapúam now hears only the vengeance-cry. The stranger shall die."

" The daughter of Araken is stronger than the Chief of warriors," said Iraçéma, seizing the war-trumpet.[2] " She holds here the voice of the Tupan-god, who calls on his people."

" But she will *not* call," said the Chief scoffingly.

" No, because Irapúam shall be punished by the hand of Iraçéma. His first step will be the step of death."

The virgin with one bound retreated as much as she had advanced and drew her bow. The chief still grasped the handle of his formidable tomahawk, but he felt for the first time that it was heavy for his strong arm. The blow that was about to strike Iraçéma had already wounded his own heart. He then knew how easily the strongest brave is, out of his very strength, vanquished by love.

" The shadow of Iraçéma will not always hide the stranger from the vengeance of Irapúam. Vile is the warrior who allows himself to be protected by a woman."

Thus saying, the Chief vanished amongst the trees. The virgin, always on the watch, returned to the

---

[1] *Goaná*, a large species of wild duck.
[2] In the original *Inubia*, a war-trumpet of large size.

sleeping Christian, and guarded him for the rest of
the night. The emotions so lately undergone agitated
her soul, and ripened all those sweet affections of her
heart which the stranger's eyes had quickened to life.

She longed to protect him from all peril, to shelter
him as though she were an impenetrable asylum.
Then, deeds following her thoughts, she passed her
arms round the sleeping warrior's neck and she pil-
lowed his head upon her bosom.

But when the joy of seeing the stranger saved from
the perils of the night had passed away, the thought
of new dangers about to arise caused her the liveliest
disquiet.

"The love of Iraçéma is like the wind of the
desert-sands; it kills the flower of the forest," sighed
the virgin.

And slowly she withdrew.

CHAPTER VIII.

THE white gleam of dawn awoke the day and opened
the eyes of the white warrior. The morning light
dissolved the visions of the night and drew from his
mind the remembrance of his dream. There remained but a vague sensation, as the perfume of the
cactus clings to the forest clump, even after the sharp
wind from the mountains has laid it bare in the
early morn.

He did not know where he was.

Leaving the sacred grove, he met Iraçéma. The
virgin was leaning against a rough trunk in the holt.
Her eyes were on the ground; the colour had fled
her cheeks, and her heart trembled upon her lip,
like drops of dew on the bamboo [1] frond.

---

[1] *Bambú*, the well-known Indian cane.

No smile, no freshness, had the Indian maid; no buds, no flowers, has the acacia scorched by the sun; no azure, no stars, has the night when loud jars the wind.

"The forest bloom has opened to the sun-ray; the birds have already sang," said the warrior. "Why does only Iraçéma hang her head and remain silent?"

The daughter of the Pagé trembled. Thus trembles the green palm when its bole is shaken; thus the rain-tears are showered from its frond; thus its fans quietly murmur.

"Cauby the brave is coming to the Taba of his brothers. The stranger can depart with the now rising sun."

"Iraçéma then would see the stranger go from the prairies of the Tabajára; then will gladness return to her heart?"

"The Juruty-dove[1] abandons the nest wherein she was born when the tree decays. No more shall joy visit the breast of Iraçéma. She will remain like the bare trunk, without branches, without shade."

Martim supported the trembling form of the maiden; she rested wearily upon the warrior's bosom, like the young tendril of the Baúnilha which twines tenderly round the sturdy branch of the Angico-acacia.[2]

The youth murmured—

"Thy guest remains, maid with the black eyes! he stays to bring back upon thy cheek the flower of happiness, and to sip like the bee the honey of thy lips."

Iraçéma disengaged herself from the youth's arms and looked at him with sadness.

"White warrior! Iraçéma is the daughter of the Pagé, and keeps the secret of the Juréma draught. The brave that shall possess the Virgin of Tupan will die.

---

[1] *Juruty*, a species of Brazilian dove.
[2] *Angico*, a large cedar much prized by joiners and carpenters.

"And Iraçéma?"

"If thou shouldst die!" . . .

This word was a sigh of agony. The youth's head fell upon his breast, but soon he raised his form.

"The warriors of my race carry death with them, daughter of the Tabajáras! They do not fear it for themselves; they do not spare it to their foes. But never, unless in combat, do they leave open the Camocim[1] of the maiden in the wigwam of their host. Truth hath spoken by the mouth of Iraçéma. The stranger should leave the Tabajára camp."

"He should," said the maiden, like an echo.

Then her voice sighed forth—

"The honey of Iraçéma's lips is like the honey-comb which the bee makes in the trunk of the Guabiroba:[2] poisonous is its sweetness. The maiden with the blue eyes and sunny hair[3] keeps for her brave in the Taba of the pale-faces the honey of the lily."

Martim withdrew quickly and returned but slowly. A word trembled on his lips.

"The guest will go, that peace may return to Iraçéma's bosom."

"And he bears with him the light of Iraçéma's eyes and the flower of her soul."

A strange noise re-echoed through the forest. The youth's glance sped in its direction.

"It is Cauby the brave's cry of joy," said the maid. "Iraçéma's brother announces his safe return to the prairies of the Tabajára."

"Daughter of Araken, conduct thy guest to the wigwam. It is time to depart."

[1] *Camocim*, also called *Camotim*, the urn or chest which served as coffin to the aborigines. The word *c' am 'otim* means "hole to bury the dead," f.om *co*, hole, *ambyra*, dead, and *anhotim*, to bury.

[2] In the original *Guabiroba* or *Andiroba*, a tree which gives a pungent, bitter oil.

[3] Portuguese, *cabellos do sol*, hair like the sun; in Tupy, *guaraciába*; so they called the yellow hair of Europeans.

They paced side by side, like two fawns who at the sunset hour return through the wood to their nighting-place, whence the scent of suspicion is borne by the breeze. When they reached the Joazeiros, they saw Cauby crossing beyond them, his broad shoulders bending under the weight of his chase. Iraçéma went to meet him.

The stranger entered the wigwam alone.

CHAPTER IX.

THE morning sleep weighed down the eyelids of the Pagé like the fair-weather mists hang at daybreak over the deep caverns in the mountain-side. Martim hesitated, but the sound of his step reached the old man's ear and startled his decrepit frame.

"Araken sleeps!" murmured the warrior, slackening his pace.

The venerable Pagé remained motionless.

"The Pagé slumbers because Tupan hath turned his face to the Earth, and the Light hath frightened away the evil spirits of Darkness. But sleep sits lightly on the eyes of Araken, like the smoke of the Sapé-grass [1] on the top of the Serra. If the stranger came to see the Pagé, speak; his ears are open."

"The guest came to tell Araken that he is about to go forth."

"The stranger is Lord in the wigwam of Araken; all the roads are open to him. May Tupan guide him to the Taba of his race."

Cauby and Iraçéma came up.

"Cauby has returned," said the Tabajára brave. "He brings to Araken the best of his game."

---

[1] *Sapé*, leaves for thatch; coarse grass which grows on worn-out lands.

"The warrior Cauby is a mighty huntsman of the mountains and the forests. The eyes of his father are proud to dwell upon him."

The old man opened his eyes, but they soon closed again.

"Daughter of Araken! choose for thy guest the Return Gift, and prepare the Moquem [1] for the journey. If the stranger need a guide, Cauby, the Lord of the Path,[2] will accompany him."

And sleep once more closed his eyes.

While Cauby hung up the quarry over the smoke, Iraçéma took her own white hammock of cotton fringed with feathers, and folded it into the Urú of plaited straw.

Martim awaited her at the doorway of the wigwam, and the maiden came to him and said—

"Warrior that takest away the sleep from Iraçéma's eyes, take also her hammock. When he sleeps in it, may dreams of Iraçéma speak with his heart."

"Thy hammock, maiden of the Tabajáras, shall be my companion in the wilds. Let the cold wind of night blow fiercely, it will protect the stranger with its warmth and breathe the sweet perfume of Iraçéma's bosom."

Cauby went forth to see his wigwam, which he had not visited since his return. Iraçéma departed to prepare provisions for the voyage. There remained in the cabin only the Pagé, who was sleeping aloud, and the youth with his sorrows.

The sun was setting when Iraçéma's brother returned from the great wigwam.

---

[1] *Moquem*, in the original, from *mocaem*. The Brazilian Indians roasted their game before a bright fire to prevent its putrefying when they took it on a journey, and in their tents they hung it over the smoke.

[2] *Senhor do caminho*, "Lord of the Path," is what the aborigines called their guide.

"The day ends sadly,"[1] quoth Cauby. "The night-shade is already falling. It is time to depart."

The virgin laid her hand gently on the hammock of Araken.

"He goes," murmured her trembling lips.

The Pagé stood upright in the midst of the wigwam and lit his Calumet. He and the youth exchanged the pipe of farewell.

"Well-go[2] the Guest, even as he was welcome to the wigwam of Araken."

The old man walked to the door and puffed forth a cloud of smoke upon the wind. When it had dispersed in thin air he said—

"May the Jurupary[3] hide himself, and allow the guest of the Pagé to pass unmolested."

Araken returned to his hammock and slept again.

The youth took his arms, which seemed to be heavier than when he had first hung them to the stakes round the wigwam, and prepared to depart.

First went Cauby; at some little distance followed the stranger, and directly after him Iraçéma.

They descended the hill and entered the dark forest. Already the Sabiá of the wold, sweetest songster of eventide, deep hidden in the thick myrtle-brake,[4] warbled the prelude of her plaintive song.

The virgin sighed forth—

"The evening is the Sorrow of the Sun. The days of Iraçéma will be long evenings without a morn, until the Shadow of the Great Night shall fall upon her."

---

[1] *O dia vae ficar triste.* The Tupys called evening *Caruca*, a word composed of "Che carac acy," "I am sad." They drew their image of grief from the twilight and the approaching gloom.

[2] In Portuguese they can say, "Well-gone be the guest as his welcoming;" but we have no single English word as a pendant to welcome.

[3] *Jurupary*, a demon, which word literally means "crooked mouth" (*juru*, a mouth, and *apara*, crooked, deformed).

[4] In the original *Ubaia*, a myrtle with a healthy wholesome fruit (*uba*, a fruit, and *aia*, good).

The youth turned towards her. His lip was silent, but his eyes spoke. One tear coursed down his manly cheek, like the drops which during the summer heat trickle over the scarped rock.

Cauby walked on and disappeared in the dense foliage.

The bosom of Araken's daughter heaved like the overflowing billow fringed with surf, and she sobbed aloud. But in her soul, so dark with sorrow, burned a faint spark which lit up her cheeks. Thus in the blackness of night a firedrake glimmers over the white sands of the high-land plateau.

"Stranger, take the last smile of Iraçéma—and fly!"

The warrior caught her in his arms and placed his lips to hers. They were as twin fruits of the Araça [1] shrub, both sprung from the womb of the same flower.

The voice of Cauby called the stranger by name, and Iraçéma remained clinging for support to the trunk of a palm.

CHAPTER X.

IN the silent wigwam meditates the old Pagé.

Iraçéma leans against the rugged trunk that serves as a stay. Her large black eyes, fixed on the forest clearings, and sunk with sorrow, gaze with long and tremulous looks, threading and unthreading the seed-pearl of teardrops that bedew her cheeks.

The Ará, perched on the opposite shelf, views with sad green eyes her beautiful lady.

From the day that saw the white warrior tread Tabajára land she had been forgotten by Iraçéma. The rosy lips of the maid never opened now to let

---

[1] *Araça*, a Brazilian shrub with fruit of the guava family.

her pick from them the fruity pulp or the paste of green maize,[1] nor ever now did the sweet hand caress her or smooth the golden plumage of her head.

If she spoke the beloved name of her mistress, the smile of Iraçéma was never bent upon her, nor did the ear of the mistress even appear to know the voice of that companion and friend, which had once been so dear to her heart.

Woe to her! The Tupy nation called her Jandáia,[2] because in her joy she made the plains resound with her vibrating song. But now, sad and silent because disdained by her mistress, she appeared no more the beautiful Jandáia, but rather the homely Urutão,[3] which knows only to groan.

Low sloped the sun over the Serra heights; its rays hardly gilded the highest crests. The hushed melancholy of evening which precedes the silence of night began to oppress the various sounds of the prairie. Here and there a night-bird, deceived by the thicker darkness of the forest, screeched aloud.

The old man raised his bald forehead.

"Was it not the cry of the Inhuma bird[4] that awoke the ear of Araken?" said he, wondering.

The maiden trembled. Already she was out of the wigwam, and back to answer the Pagé's question.

"It is the War-cry of Cauby the brave!"

When the second screech of the midnight bird

---

[1] Indian-corn, *milho.*

[2] *Jandáia,* also written *Nhendáia* and *Nhándaia,* which is an adjective that qualifies the ará or macaw, from *nheng,* to speak, *antan,* hard, rough, strong, and *ará,* the agent who acts, *nh'ant'-ará.* *Ceará* in Tupy means "the song of the jandáia," from *cemo,* to sing loud, and *arára,* paroquet.

[3] *Urutão,* a night-bird.

[4] *Inhuma,* a bird which sings regularly about midnight with a harsh unpleasant note. The orthography is *anhuma,* from *anho,* solitary, and *anum,* a well-known aotophagus, which the aborigines regarded as a bird of augury. Thus it would mean the "solitary *anum,*" the unicorn-bird.

reached her ear, Iraçéma ran towards the forest, fleet as a doe pursued by the hunter: she never drew breath till she had reached the clearing, which lay in the wood like a long lake.

The first thing that met her eye was Martim, sitting tranquilly upon a Sapopema [1] bough and eyeing all that occurred. Opposite him a hundred Tabajára warriors with Irapúam at their head formed a circle. The brave Cauby, his eye flashing with anger and his weapons grasped in his muscular arm, stood up before them all.

Irapúam had demanded the stranger, and the guide had answered him simply—

"Slay Cauby first."

The daughter of the Pagé flew like an arrow. Behold her graceful form shielding Martim from the blows of the braves. Irapúam roared with rage, as roars the ounce attacked in its lair.

"Daughter of Araken," said Cauby in a whisper, "lead the stranger to the wigwam. Araken alone can save him."

Iraçéma turned towards the white warrior.

"Come!"

He remained immovable.

"If the stranger will not come, Iraçéma will die with him."

Martim arose; but far from following the maiden, he walked straight towards Irapúam. His sword flashed in the air.

"Chief! the Braves of my race have never refused combat. If he whom thou beholdest did not seek it, it was because his fathers have forbidden him to shed blood in the land of hospitality."

The Tabajára chief yelled with joy; his powerful arm wielded the tomahawk. But the two champions

---

[1] *Sapopema,* a tree with thick branches. The wood is hard, and is much prized for furniture.

had scanty time to measure each other with the eye.
When the first blow was being struck, Cauby and
Iraçéma were between them.

In vain the daughter of Araken besought the Christian. Vainly did she throw her arms round him, en-
deavouring to withdraw him from the combat. On
his side, Cauby as vainly strove to provoke Irapúam,
and to draw upon himself the wrath of the chief.

At a sign from Irapúam, the warriors seized the
brother and sister, and the combat began.

Suddenly the hoarse sound of the War-trumpet
thundered through the forest. The sons of the Serra
trembled as they recognised the boom of the Sea-
shell and the War-cry of the Pytiguáras, those Lords
of the Shores, which the fallen trees shade. The
echo came from the Great Wigwam, which perhaps
the enemy was at that moment attacking.

The warriors flew there, carrying with them their
Chiefs. With the stranger only remained the daughter
of Araken.

CHAPTER XI.

THE Tabajára warriors, rushing to the Taba, awaited
the enemy in part of the Caiçára or Curral.[1]

The foe not coming, they went forth to seek him.

They beat the forests all around and scoured the
plains. There was no trace of the Pytiguáras; yet
the well-known War-boom of the Shell from the shores
had sounded in the ears of the mountain braves. Of
this none doubted.

Irapúam suspected that it was a stratagem of the
daughter of Araken to save the stranger, and he went

---

[1] *Caiçara,* from *cai,* a bit of burnt wood, and the desinence
çara, what *is* or is made. "What is made of burnt wood,"
i.e., a strong enclosure of pointed stakes—a Curral.

straight to the wigwam of the Pagé; as the Guará[1] runs along the skirts of the forest when following the trail of the escaping prey, so did the wrathful warrior hurry his steps.

Araken saw the great Tabajára chief enter his cabin, but he did not move. Sitting on his hammock with crossed legs, he was giving ear to Iraçéma. The maiden related the events of the evening; beholding the sinister countenance of Irapúam, she sprang to her bow and placed herself by the white warrior's side.

Martim put her gently away and advanced a few steps.

The protection with which the Tabajára maid surrounded *him*, a warrior, annoyed him.

"Araken! the vengeance of the Tabajáras demands the white warrior; Irapúam comes to fetch him."

"The Guest is the beloved of Tupan; who so molests the Stranger shall hear the voice of his Thunder."

"It is the Stranger who has offended Tupan, robbing him of his Virgin who keeps the dreams of the Juréma draught."

"The mouth of Irapúam lies like the hiss of the Giboia,"[2] exclaimed Iraçéma.

Martim said—

"Irapúam is vile, and unworthy to be the Chief of braves."

The Pagé spoke slow and solemnly—

"If the Virgin has yielded the flower of her Chastity to the white warrior, she will die; but the Guest of

---

[1] *Guará*, a wild dog, the Brazilian wolf. The word decomposed with *g*, the relative *u*, to eat, and *ara* for *a*, the emphatic desinence is *g-u-ára*, "comedor," or "voracious eater."

[2] *Giboia*, the wild people so called the boa-constrictor, the largest snake in the Brazils, which can easily swallow a stag. The word comes from *gi*, a hatchet, and *boia*, any snake (the root of our "boa"), because the serpent strikes with its fangs like the blow of a hatchet.

Tupan is sacred; none shall touch him; all shall serve him."

Irapúam raged; his hoarse growl rumbled within his muscular chest like the noise made by the Sucury [1] in the depths of the river.

"The wrath of Irapúam's anger will not let him hearken to the old Pagé! It will fall upon *him* if he dare to withdraw the Stranger from the vengeance of the Tabajáras."

At this moment the venerable Andíra, brother of the Pagé, entered the cabin. He grasped the terrible tomahawk, and a still more terrible fury gleamed in his eyes.

"The vampire comes to suck Irapúam's blood, if indeed it *is* blood and not honey [2] that runs in the veins of him who dares to threaten the old Pagé in his wigwam."

Araken stayed his brother.

"Peace and silence, Andíra!"

The Pagé raised his tall thin stature, and appeared like the angry viper [3] who crouches on the ground the better to spring upon his victim. His wrinkles waxed deeper, whilst his shrunken lips displayed his white and sharpened teeth.

"Let Irapúam venture one step more, and the wrath of Tupan shall crush him with the weight of this lean and withered hand!"

"At this moment Tupan is not with the Pagé," replied the Chief.

The Pagé laughed, and the sinister laugh seemed

---

[1] *Sucury* or *Sucurin*, a gigantic serpent which lies in deep rivers, and can swallow an ox. The word comes from *suu*, an animal, and *cury* or *curu*, a snorter, "the snorting or hissing beast."

[2] *Si é que tens sangue e não mel nas veias.* The meaning of the word *Irapúam* is "round honey." It must be remembered that Irapúam taunted Andira farther back about *his* name, which means "old vampire," and this was *his* retort.

[3] In the original *Caninana*.

to roll round the enclosure like the bark of the Ariranha.[1]

"Hear his thunder,[2] and let the warrior's soul tremble as the earth in its depths!"

Araken pronouncing these terrible words, advanced to the middle of the wigwam. There he lifted up a great stone and stamped with force upon the ground, which suddenly clave asunder. A frightful noise, which seemed torn from the bowels of the earth, issued out from the dark cavern.

Irapúam neither trembled nor turned pale, but he felt his sight growing dim and his lips lost their power of speech.

"The Lord of Thunder is for the Pagé; the Lord of War will be for Irapúam."

The grim warrior left the wigwam, and soon his mighty form disappeared in the twilight.

The Pagé and his brother resumed their conversation in the doorway.

Martim, still surprised at what he had beheld, could not take his eyes off the deep cavern, which the stamp of the old Pagé had opened in the ground. A dull sound, like the distant boom of the waves breaking upon the shore, still echoed through the depths.

The Christian warrior reflected; he could not believe that the God of the Tabajáras had given such immense power to his priest.

Araken perceiving what was passing in the mind of the stranger, lit the Caximbo and seized the Maracá, or mystic rattle.

---

[1] *Ariranha*, the largest species of Brazilian otter.

[2] *Ouve seu trovão.* This was a stratagem practised by the Pagés to rule their votaries by terror. The hut was built upon a rock which contained a subterraneous passage, communicating by a narrow aperture with the plain. Araken had taken the precaution to block up the two entrances with stones, and thus to hide them from the people. Removing one stone from each end caused the air to rush through the narrow spiral channel with a loud noise, as the sea-shell murmurs when applied to the ear.

"It is time," he said, "to appease the wrath of Tupan and to hush the voice of his thunder."

So saying he left the cabin.

Iraçéma then approached the youth with laughing mouth and eyes sparkling with joy.

"The heart of Iraçéma is like the rice-plant, glad in the waves of the river.[1] None can hurt the white warrior in the wigwam of Araken."

"Keep away from the enemy, Tabajára maid," replied the stranger in a harsh voice. And retiring quickly to the opposite side of the wigwam, he hid his face from the tender complaining looks of the virgin.

"What has Iraçéma done that the white warrior should turn away his eyes from her as if she were the worm of the earth?"

The maiden's words, gently whispered, reached Martim's heart. Thus whisper the murmurs of the breeze in the fan-leaves of the palm-tree. The youth felt anger against himself and sorrow for her.

"Dost thou not hear, beautiful virgin?" exclaimed he, pointing to the speaking cave.

"It is the voice of Tupan!"

"Thy god speaks by the mouth of his Pagé: *If the virgin of Tupan yield to the stranger the flower of her chastity, she shall die.*"

Iraçéma hung her head.

"It is not the voice of Tupan that the pale-faced warrior hears, but the song of the white virgin that calls to him."

Suddenly the strange sounds which came from the depths of the earth ceased, and there was so deep a silence in the wigwam, that the pulses throbbing through the warrior's veins and the sighs that trembled on the virgin's lips were heard.

---

[1] In the original *abati*, or *abaty n'agua. Abati* is rice, which thrives when in water, and which Iraçéma used as a symbol of her joy.

CHAPTER XII.

THE day darkened ; night was already coming on.

The Pagé returned to the wigwam, and again poising the slab of stone, closed with it the mouth of the subterranean passage.

Cauby also arrived from the great Taba, where he and his brother braves had retired after beating the forest in search of the Pytiguara enemy.

In the centre of the wigwam, amidst the hammocks, slung and squared, Iraçéma spread the mat of Carnaúba palm, and served the remains of the game with the wines made during the last moon. The Tabajára brave alone relished the supper ; the gall which is wrung from the heart by sorrow did not embitter his palate.

The Pagé drew from his calumet the sacred smoke of Tupan, which filled the depths of his lungs. The stranger greedily inhaled the fresh air to cool his boiling blood. The maiden seemed to sigh her soul away, like honey dropping from the comb, in the frequent sobs that burst from her trembling lips.

Cauby soon retired to the great Taba ; the Pagé still inhaled the smoke which prepared him for the mysteries of the Sacred Rite.

There arises in the night silence a vibrating cry which ascends to the sky. Martim raises up his head and listens. Again a similar sound is heard. The warrior whispers, so that only the maiden could hear him—

" Hast heard, Iraçéma, the Seagull's cry ? "

" Iraçéma has heard the cry of a bird which she does not know."

" It is the Atyaty,[1] the Heron of the Sea, and Iraçéma is the mountain-maid who has never trodden upon the white beach upon which the waves break."

---

[1] *Atyaty*, seagull.

"The beach belongs to the Pytiguaras, the Lords of the Palm groves."

The warriors of the great tribe who inhabited the seaboard called themselves Pytiguaras, Lords of the Valleys; but the Tabajáras, their enemies, contemptuously termed them Potyuáras, or Shrimp-Eaters.

Iraçéma did not wish to offend the white warrior, and therefore, when speaking of the Pytiguaras, she gave them the warlike name which they had chosen for themselves.

The stranger reflected, and retained for a moment, on the lip of prudence, the word which he was about to utter.

"The Seagull's song is the War-cry of the brave Poty, the friend of thy guest."

The maiden trembled for her brethren. The fame of the fierce Poty, brother of Jacaúna, had spread afar, from the sea-shore to the heights of the Serra. Scarcely was there a wigwam which had not panted with a lust of vengeance; in almost all of them the blow of his unerring tomahawk had laid a warrior low in his Camocim.

Iraçéma thought that Poty came at the head of his braves to deliver his friend. Doubtless it was he who had sounded the Sea-shell at the time when the combat began. It was therefore in a tone of mixed sadness and sweetness that she replied—

"The stranger is saved; the brethren of Iraçéma will die, for she will not speak."

"Cast out this grief from thy soul, Tabajára maid! The stranger in leaving thy prairies will not leave in them, like the famished tiger, a trail of blood."

Iraçéma took the hand of the white warrior and kissed it.

"The stranger's smile," she continued, "blunts the remembrance of the harm they wish me."

Martim rose and walked to the door.

"Where goes the white warrior?"

" To seek Poty."

" The guest of Araken may not leave this wigwam, for the warriors of Irapúam will kill him."

" A warrior owes his life to God and to his weapons only. He will not be protected by old men and women ! "

" What is one brave against a thousand ? The Tamanduá[1] is brave and strong, yet the cats of the mountains kill and eat him because they are so many. The arms of the white warrior only reach as far as the shadow of his body—those of the Tabajáras fly high and straight as the Anajé."[2]

" Every warrior has his day."

" The stranger would not see Iraçéma die, yet he would make her behold his death."

Martim hesitated, perplexed.

" Iraçéma will go and meet the Pytiguára Chief, and will bring to her guest the words of his warrior friend."

The Pagé finally awoke from his reverie. The Maracá rattled in his right hand ; the bells rang in time to his stiff slow step.

He called his daughter apart.

" If the braves of Trapúam fall upon the wigwam, lift up the stone and hide the stranger in the bosom of the earth."

" The guest must not be left alone. Wait till Iraçéma returns. The inhuma has not yet sung."

The old man again sat upon his hammock. The maiden went forth after fastening the door of the wigwam.

[1] *Tamanduá*, ant-eater.
[2] *Anajé*, a powerful hawk, the local eagle.

CHAPTER XIII.

THE daughter of Araken advances in the darkness; she stands and listens. For the third time the cry of the Seagull sounds in her ears; she bends her steps straight to the place whence it came, and arrives at the edge of a lake. Her glance pierces the darkness, but finds nought of what it seeks. The tender voice, soft as the hum of the colibri bird, breaks the silence.

"Poty, the brave's white brother calls him by the mouth of Iraçéma!"

Echo only answered her.

"The Daughter of his Foes comes to seek him, because the stranger loves him, and she loves the stranger."

The smooth surface of the lake clove, and a figure appeared swimming towards the margin and rising from the water.

"Was it Martim who sent Iraçéma, since she knows the name of Poty, his brother in war?"

"The Pytiguára chief may speak; the white warrior is waiting."

"Then Iraçéma will return and tell him that Poty has come to save him."

"The stranger knows, and sent Iraçéma to hear Poty's tidings."

"The words of Poty will leave his mouth only for the ear of his white brother."

"He must wait then till Araken leaves and the wigwam remains deserted; then will Iraçéma guide him to the presence of the stranger."

"Never, daughter of the Tabajáras! has a Pytiguára brave crossed the threshold of a foeman's wigwam save as a conqueror. Bring here the warrior of the sea."

"The vengeance of Irapúam hovers around the wigwam of Araken. Has the stranger's brother brought Pytiguára warriors enough to defend and to save him ? "

Poty reflected.

"Relate, Maid of the Mountains, all that has happened in these prairies since the Warrior of the Sea planted foot upon them."

Iraçéma related all—how the wrath of Irapúam had burst forth against the stranger, until the voice of Tupan, invoked by the Pagé, had appeased his fury.

"The anger of Irapúam is like that of the bat ; he fears the light and flies only in the dark."

The hand of Poty suddenly closed the maiden's lips ; his words sank to a whisper.

"The Virgin of the Forest must hold her breath and hush her voice ; the foeman's ear listens in the dark."

The leaves gently rustled as if trodden upon by the restless Nambú. The sound at first came from the skirts of the forest and then swept towards the valley. The valiant Poty gliding along the grass, like the clever prawn from which he took his name and quickness, disappeared in the deep lake. The water without a murmur buried him in its limpid wave.

Iraçéma returned to the wigwam ; on the way she perceived the shadows of many warriors who were crawling on the ground like the Intanha frog.[1]

Araken, seeing her come in, left the wigwam.

The Tabajára maid related to Martim all that had passed between herself and Poty. The Christian warrior rose up impetuously to rescue his Pytiguára brother. Iraçéma threw round his neck her beautiful arms.

"The Chief does not want his brother. He is the son of the waters, and the waters will protect him. Later, the stranger's ear shall listen to the words of his friend."

---

[1] *Intanha*, commonly called the *ferrador*, the blacksmith frog.

" Iraçéma, it is time that thy guest should leave the wigwam of the Pagé and the plains of the Tabajáras. He does not fear the braves of Irapúam ; he fears the eyes of the Virgin of Tupan."

" He will fly from them ? "

" The stranger *must* fly from *them* as the Oitibó does from the morning star."

Martim hastened his steps.

"Ungrateful brave ! go slay, first brother, then self. Iraçéma will follow him to the happy plains where wend the shades of those that were."

" Kill my brother, sayest thou, cruel maid ? "

"Thy trail will guide the enemy to his hiding-place."

The Christian halted suddenly midway in the wigwam, and there remained silent and still. Iraçéma, fearing to look upon him, fixed her eyes on his shadow, which the bright embers of the fire threw on the broken wall of the wigwam.

The shaggy dog lying close to the hot ashes gave signs that a friend was approaching. The door interwoven with the fronds of the Carnaúba palm was opened from without. Cauby entered.

" The Cauim wine has disturbed the spirit of the braves. They are coming to slay the stranger."

The maiden arose impetuously.

"Lift up the stone which closes the throat of Tupan, that he may conceal the guest."

The Tabajára brave uphove the enormous slab, and poised it on the ground.

" The son of Araken shall lie across the Wigwam-door, and if a brave pass over his body, let him rise no more from the ground."

Cauby obeyed. The maiden fastened the door.

A few moments passed. The war-cry of the braves sounds closer ; the angry voices of Irapúam and Cauby rise above the rest.

" They come, but Tupan will save his guest."

At this moment, as if the thunder-god had heard the words of his virgin, the cave, which till then was still, roared with a dull roar.

"Listen! It is the voice of Tupan!"

Iraçéma presses the warrior's hand and leads him into the cave. They descend together into the bowels of the earth.

CHAPTER XIV.

THE Tabajára braves, excited by their copious libations of foaming Cauim, were inflamed by the voice of Irapúam, who had so often led them to victory.

Wine appeases the thirst of the body, but breeds another and a wilder thirst in the savage mind.

The braves yell vengeance against the audacious stranger who had defied their arms, and who had offended the God of their fathers and their War Chief, the greatest of the Tabajáras.

Then they leapt with rage and rushed about in the darkness. The red light of the Ubirátán[1] which shone in the distance guided them to the cabin of Araken.

From time to time the foremost of those who came to spy the enemy raised themselves up from the ground.

"The Pagé is in the forest," they murmured.

"And the stranger?" inquired Irapúam.

"In the cabin with Iraçéma."

The great chief leaps up with a terrific bound, and reaches the Wigwam-door followed by his warriors.

The face of Cauby appears at the entrance. His arms guarded a space in front of him—say within the reach of a Maracajá's spring.[2]

[1] The iron wood of *ubira* (from *pái*, wood, and *antan*, hard).

[2] *Maracajá* is a wild cat. It must not be confounded with

" Dastardly are the braves who attack in herds like the Caetetús.[1]   The Jaguar,[2] Lord of the Forest, and the Anajê, Lord of the Clouds, combat the enemy alone."

" Dirt be in the vile mouth which raises its voice against the bravest of the Tabajára braves."

Saying these words, Irapúam brandished his fatal tomahawk, but his arm stopped in the air.   The bowels of the earth again rumbled as they had rumbled when Araken awoke the awful voice of Tupan.

The braves raise a cry of fear, and, surrounding their Chief, force him away from the funest spot and the wrath of Tupan, so evidently roused against them.

Cauby once more lay down across the threshold ; his eyes sleep but his ears keep watch.

The voice of Tupan became silent.

Iraçéma and the Christian, lost in the depths of the earth, descended into a deep grotto.   Suddenly a voice arising from the cavernous depths filled their ears.

" Does the Sea-Warrior listen to the words of his brother ? "

" It is Poty, the friend of thy guest," said the Christian to the maid.

Iraçéma trembled.

" He speaks by the mouth of Tupan."

Martim then answered the Pytiguára—

"The words of Poty enter into the soul of his brother."

the *Maracujá* or passion-flower, which represents all the instruments of our Saviour's passion, as the pillar, nails, scourges, and crown of thorns.

[1] *Caetetús* is the wild pig of the forest, from *caeté*, large virgin forest, and *sun*, game, which euphony changes to *tu*.

[2] *Jaguar*, amongst the aborigines, was applied to all the animals that devoured them, especially the ounce. *Jaguareté* meant "the great eater."   It is derived from *ja*, "us," and *guara*, "the voracious."

" Does no other ear listen ? "

" None save those of the Virgin who twice in one sun has saved the life of thy brother."

" Woman is weak ; the Tabajára is revengeful ; and the brother of Jacaúna [1] is prudent."

Iraçéma sighed and lay her head upon the youth's breast.

" Lord of Iraçéma, stop her ears that she may not listen."

Martim gently put away the graceful head.

" The Pytiguára Chief may speak ; the ears that listen are friendly and faithful."

" His brother orders and Poty speaks. Ere the sun shall rise over the Serra, the Sea-Warrior must seek the river-plain of the Herons' Nests. The Dead Star will guide him to the white beach. No Tabajára brave will follow him, because the Inubia of the Pytiguáras will sound from the mountain-side."

" How many Pytiguára braves accompany their valiant Chief ? "

" Not one. Poty came alone with his arms. When the bad spirits of the forest separated the Sea-Warrior from his brother, Poty followed his trail. His heart would not let him return to call the braves of his Taba ; but he sent his faithful dog to the great Jacaúna."

" The Pytiguára Chief is alone ; he must not sound the Inubia, which will raise all the Tabajára braves against him."

" He *must* do it to save his white brother. Poty will mock at Irapúam, as he mocked him when he fought with a hundred men against his white brother."

The daughter of the Pagé, who had listened silently, now bent towards the Christian's ear.

" Iraçéma would save the stranger and his brother ; she knows her thoughts. The Pytiguára Chief is

---

[1] *Jacaúna* was the celebrated Chief, brother of Poty, and a friend to Martim Soares Moreno. His name is that of a black tree, also called in Brazil Jacarandá.

staunch and brave. Irapúam is crafty and treacherous as the Acauan.[1] Before the stranger can reach the forest he must fall, and his brother must also fall with him."

"What can the Tabajára maid do to save the stranger and his brother?" asked Martim.

"One more sun and another must rise, then the moon of flowers[2] will appear. It is the feast-time when the Tabajára braves pass the night in the Sacred Wood and receive from the Pagé their happy dreams. When they are all sleeping, the white warrior will leave the plains of Ipú, and will vanish from the eyes of Iraçéma, but not from her soul."

Martim strained the maiden to his breast, but soon he gently repelled her. The contact of her beautiful form, sweet as the forest lily, warm as the nest of the Beijaflor,[3] was as a thorn in his heart. He remembered the awful warning of the Pagé.

The voice of the Christian repeated to Poty the project of Iraçéma; the Pytiguára chief, prudent as the Tamanduá, took thought, and then replied—

"Wisdom has spoken by the mouth of the Tabajára Virgin. Poty will wait the moon of flowers."

CHAPTER XV.

THE day was born and dead. The fire, companion of the night, already shone in the Wigwam of Araken. The stars, daughters of the moon, rolled their slow and silent courses in the blue heavens, awaiting the return of their absent mother.

---

[1] The *Acauan* is a Secretary-bird that destroys serpents. The word is from *caa*, wood, and *uan*, from *u*, " to eat "—a wood-eater.

[2] *A lua das flores*, the moon of flowers.

[3] *Beijaflor*, literally Kiss-flower, the humming-bird.

Martim gently rocked himself; and his soul, like the white hammock which waved from side to side, wavered between one and another thought. There the pale-faced virgin awaited him with chaste affection. Here the dark maiden smiled upon him with ardent love.

Iraçéma leant languidly against the head of the hammock; her large black eyes, tender as those of the Sabiá-thrush, sought the stranger and pierced his soul. The Christian smiled. The virgin, trembling like the Sahy-bird [1] fascinated by the serpent, bent her yielding form and reclined upon the warrior's bosom.

He strained her passionately to his heart, his lips sought her longing lip, and thus they celebrated in this sanctuary of the soul the hymen of love.

In a dark obscure corner sat the Pagé, plunged in the contemplation of things remote from this world. He heaved one long sad sigh. Did his heart forebode that which his eyes could not see? Or was it some ill-omened presentiment concerning the future of his race which re-echoed in the soul of Araken?

No one ever knew!

The Christian gently repelled the Indian girl. He would not leave a trail of disgrace in the hospitable Wigwam. He closed his eyes that he might not see her, and endeavoured to fill his thoughts with the name and the fear of God.

Christ!—Jesus!—Mary!

A calm returned to the warrior's breast, but every time his eye rested upon the Tabajára virgin he felt the blood course through his veins like liquid fire. Thus when the thoughtless child stirs the live embers, its sparks fly out and consume its flesh.

The Christian shut his eyes, but amid the darkness of his thoughts the Tabajára virgin ever arose, and ever more beautiful. In vain his heavy lids invoked

---

[1] *Sahy*, a beautiful blue bird.

sleep. They opened despite all his endeavours. An inspiration from Heaven at last descended upon his troubled mind.

"Beautiful maid of the desert! this is the last night of thy guest under the roof of Araken. Would that he had never come there! For thy sake and for his own, make his sleep glad and happy."

"Let the warrior command, and Iraçéma will obey. What can she do to make him glad?"

The Christian murmured low that the old Pagé might not hear him.

"The Virgin of Tupan keeps the dreams of the Jurema, which are sweet and pleasant!"

A sad smile was Iraçéma's answer.

"The stranger is going to live for ever encircling the white virgin.[1] Never more will his eyes behold the daughter of Araken; yet he wishes that sleep should close his lids, and that dreams should convey him back to the land of his brothers!"

"Sleep is the warrior's rest," said Martim, "and dreams are the gladness of his soul. The stranger would not bear sadness with him from the Land of Hospitality, nor would he leave it in the heart of Iraçéma."

The virgin sat unmoved.

"Go! and return with the wine of Tupan."

When Iraçéma came back, the Pagé was no longer in the Wigwam. She drew from her bosom the bowl which she had hidden under her Carioba[2] of cotton interwoven with feathers. Martim seized it from her hands, and drained the few drops of bitter green liquid. Presently the hammock received his torpid form.

Now he may live with Iraçéma, and gather the

---

[1] In the original *á cintura da virgem.* The savages call a successful lover *aguaçaba,* which literally means, the woman whom the man's arm encircles.

[2] *Carioba,* a cotton garment ornamented with parrots' feathers.

kisses from her lips which ripened there amidst smiles, like the fruit in the corolla of the flower. He may love her, and may savour the honey and perfume of this love without leaving its poison in the virgin's breast.

The joy was life, only more real and intense. The evil was a dream, an illusion ; to him the maiden was an image, a shadow.

Iraçéma withdrew, silent and sorrowful. The warrior's arms opened, and his lips gently murmured her name.

The Juruty flitting about the forest hears the tender cooing of her mate. She flutters her wings and flies to meet him in the warm nest. Thus the virgin of the desert nestled in the warrior's arms.

When morning came, it found Iraçéma sleeping like a butterfly in the petals of the beautiful cactus. Her cheek was suffused with the blushes of modesty, and as the first sunbeam sparkles through the early dawn, on her brightened face shone the happy smile of the bride, the aurora of happy love.

Martim seeing Iraçéma still pressed to his heart, thought that the dream continued, and closed his eyes not to disturb it.

The Poçema-trump of the braves thundering through the valley awoke him from the sweet illusion. He knew then that he was alive and awake. His cruel hand smothered the kiss which expanded like a flower on the bride's lips.

" The kisses of Iraçéma are sweet in dreams. The white warrior fills his soul with them. But in life the lips of the Virgin of Tupan are bitter and painful like the Jurema-thorns."

The daughter of Araken hid her joy in her heart. She was hushed and startled like the bird which feels the coming storm. She quickly withdrew from the Wigwam, and plunged into the river according to custom.

The Jandaia never returned to the Wigwam, and Tupan no longer owned his Virgin in the Tabajára land.

CHAPTER XVI.

THE moon's white disc rose slowly above the horizon. The brightness of the sun pales the virgin of the heavens, as the warrior's love blanches the wife's cheek.

"Jacy!"[1] . . . "Our mother!" exclaimed the Tabajára warriors. And brandishing their bows, they chanted the song of the new moon, discharging at her showers of arrows.

"Thou art come into the heavens, O mother of the braves! Thou turnest thy face once more to behold thy sons. Thou bringest waters to fill the rivers, and pulp to the Cujú-nut.

"Thou art come, O bride of the sun! Thy daughters, the virgins of the earth, smile at thy approach. May thy soft light bring love into the hearts of the brave, and make fruitful the young mother's bosom."

The evening was falling. The women and children sported in the vast Ocara. The youths who had not yet won their name by notable deeds were running races in the valley.

The warriors followed Irapúam to the Sacred Wood, where the Pagé and his daughter awaited them for the mysteries of the Jurema.

Iraçéma had already lit the fires of joy![2]

----

[1] *Jacy*, the moon, literally our mother. Amongst the savages the moon was a month, and at the change they held their feast.

[2] *Fogos de alegria*. The savages called their fire-faggots *tory* and *toryba*. A joy-feast was a great number of fires.

Araken remained statue-like and ecstatic in the centre of a cloud of smoke.

Each warrior on arriving placed at his feet an offering for Tupan. One brought the succulent game, another water-flour, a third Piracem [1] of the Trahira, [2] and so on each in turn. The old Pagé, for whom were the gifts, received them with disdain.

When all had taken seat round the Great Fire, the priest of Tupan commanded silence by a gesture, and three times pronounced aloud the dread name, as though to fill himself with the God who inspired him.

" Tupan ! Tupan ! Tupan !"

Three times the distant echoes answered the name.

Iraçéma came with the Igaçaba full of the green liquor. Araken decreed to each warrior his dreams, and distributed the wine of the Jurema, which was to transport the Tabajára brave to the happy land.

The mighty hunter dreamt that stags and Pácas [3] ran to meet his arrows and transfixed themselves ; at length, tired of wounding them, he dug the Bucan [4] in the earth, and roasted so much game that a thousand warriors could not finish it in a year.

The conqueror of hearts dreamt that the most beautiful of the Tabajára virgins left their fathers' Wigwams to follow him, slaves to his will and pleasure. Never had the hammock of any chief witnessed the reality of such wild warm visions.

The hero's vision was of tremendous struggles and fearful combats, whence he always issued victorious and covered with fame and glory.

[1] In the original *farinha d'agua.* This is a sort of flour like tapioca, which the Indians used to eat mixed with water.

[2] *Piracem de trahira.* Trahira is a river fish. *Pira caém* means fish roasted.

[3] *Pácas (Cavia páca),* a small rodent in Brazil like a pig two months old ; its flesh is eaten.

[4] *Bucan* is a Tupy word for a way of grilling flesh, which the French of Maranhão turn into *boucaner,* and whence comes our English *buccaneer.*

The old man saw his youth renewed in his numerous offspring, like the dry trunk acquiring new strength and sap, and still sprouting into buds and flowers.

All felt such lively, such lasting happiness, that in one night they lived many moons.

Their lips murmured, their gestures spoke; and the Pagé, who saw and heard all, gathered from their unveiled souls their most secret thoughts.

When Iraçéma had offered to each brave the wine of Tupan, she left the wood. The rites did not permit her to be present at the sleep of the warriors, nor hear and see their dreams.

She went her way straight to the cabin, where Martim awaited her.

"Let the white warrior take up his arms. It is time to go."

"Lead me to my brother Poty."

The bride made straight for the valley, the Christian following her. They reached the rock base, which fell sloping with clumps of foliage upon the margin of the lake.

"Let the stranger call his brother."

Martim imitated the cry of the seagull.

The stone which closed the entrance of the grotto fell, and the figure of Poty the brave appeared in the gloom.

The two brothers pressed forehead to forehead and breast to breast, showing that they had but one heart.

"Poty is happy because he sees his brother, whom the bad spirit of the forest had borne away from his sight."

"Happy is the brave who has a friend at his side like the valiant Poty; all the other warriors will envy him."

Iraçéma sighed, thinking that the affection of the Pytiguára sufficed to the happiness of the stranger.

"The Tabajára braves sleep. The daughter of Araken will guide the strangers."

D

The bride led the way; the two warriors followed behind. When they had gone about the distance of a heron's flight, the Pytiguára chief began to be uneasy, and whispered in the ear of the Christian—

"My brother had better send the daughter of the Pagé back to the Wigwam of her father. The warriors could march quicker without her."

Martim felt a sudden sadness; but the voice of prudence and friendship prevailed in his heart. He advanced to Iraçéma and spoke softly to soothe her sorrow.

"The deeper the root in the earth, the harder it is to withdraw the plant. Each step Iraçéma takes on the road of farewell is a root which she plants in the heart of her guest."

"Iraçéma would accompany him as far as the borders of the Tabajára land, in order to return with more calmness in her breast."

Martim did not answer. They continued their march, and as they walked the night fell, the stars paled, and finally the freshness of dawn gladdened the forest; the morning clouds, purely white as cotton, appeared in the heavens.

Poty looked at the forest and stopped. Martim understood, and said to Iraçéma—

"Thy guest no longer treads on the land of the Tabajáras. It is the right moment to bid him farewell."

CHAPTER XVII.

IRAÇÉMA placed her hand upon the bosom of the white warrior.

"The daughter of the Tabajáras has now left the land of her fathers, and she may speak."

"What keepest thou within thy bosom, beautiful daughter of the forest?"

She gazed with brimming eyes at the Christian.

"Iraçéma cannot tear herself from the stranger."

"Yet thus it must be, daughter of Araken. Return to the cabin of thine old father, who awaits thee."

"Araken has no longer a daughter."

Martim turned towards her with a harsh and severe gesture.

"A warrior of my race never leaves the Wigwam of his host widowed of its joy. Araken will embrace his daughter, and shall not curse the ungrateful stranger."

The girl hung her head; veiled in the long black tresses which hung about her neck, she crossed her beautiful arms over her bosom, and stood robed in her modesty. Thus the rosy cactus, before opening into a lovely flower, retains within its breast the perfumed bud.

"Thy slave will accompany thee, white warrior, because thy blood sleeps in her bosom."

Martim trembled.

"The bad spirits of the night have disturbed the spirit of Iraçéma."

"The white warrior was dreaming when Tupan abandoned his Virgin, because she betrayed the secret of the Jurema."

The Christian hid his face from the light.

"O God!" exclaimed his trembling lip.

Both remained silent.

At last Poty spoke—

"The Tabajára warriors awake."

The heart of the bride, like that of the stranger, was deaf to the voice of prudence. The sun arose in the horizon, and his majestic glance descended from the wooded uplands to the forest. Poty stood like a solitary tree-trunk waiting for his brother to give the signal for departure. It was Iraçéma who broke silence.

"Come! the life of the warrior is in danger until
he treads the Pytiguára land."

Martim followed the girl silently, and she flitted
before him amongst the trees like the timid Acoty.[1]
Sorrow preyed upon his heart, but the perfume wafted
on the air by the passage of the beautiful Tabajára
fanned the love in his warrior-breast. Still his step
was slow and his breathing was oppressed.

Poty reflected. In his youthful brain had lived the
spirit of an Abaeté.[2] The Pytiguára Chief thought
th love is like Cauim, which, drunk with moderation,
fortifies the brave, but in excess weakens the hero's
courage. He knew how fleet was the Tabajára's foot,
and he expected the moment when he must die de-
fending his friend.

As the shades of evening began to sadden the day,
the Christian stopped in the middle of the forest.
Poty lit the fire of hospitality. The bride unfolded
the white hammock of cotton fringed with the feathers
of the Toucan,[3] and hung it to the branches of a tree.

"Husband of Iraçéma, thy hammock awaits thee."

The daughter of Áraken then went and sat afar off
on the root of a tree, like the solitary doe who has
been driven forth from the sunny plain by her ungrateful mate. The Pytiguára warrior disappeared in
the thickest of the foliage.

Martim sat silent and sorrowful, like the trunk of
some tree from which the wind has torn the beautiful
Cipó [4] which embraced it. The passing breeze at last
bore on it one murmur—

"Iraçéma!"

It was the cry of the mate. The wounded doe flew
back to the sunny plain.

---

[1] *Acoty*, generally written *cutia*, a racoon.

[2] *Abaeté* means a good, strong, wise, clever man.

[3] *Tucano*, a well-known bird with gorgeous plumage, black,
green, scarlet, and orange, with a large beak.

[4] *Cipó*, a Lliana or climbing plant.

The forest distilled its sweetest fragrance and was vocal with its most harmonious music; the sighs of the heart mingled with the whispers of the wilderness. It was the feast of Love, the song of Hymen.

Already the morning light pierced the dense thicket, when the solemn and sonorous voice of Poty sounded amidst the hum and the buzz of waking life.

"The Tabajáras walk through the forest!"

Iraçéma sprang from the arms that encircled her and from the lips which held her captive—sprang from the hammock lightly to the ground, like the agile Zabelê,[1] and seizing the weapons of her spouse, led him into the depths of the bush.

From time to time the prudent Poty laid his ear to the face of earth, and his head inclined from side to side, as the cloud on the summit of a rock waves with every puff of the coming storm.

"What does the ear of the warrior Poty hear?"

"It listens to the flying step of the Tabajára. He comes like the Tapyr[2] tearing through the forest."

"The Pytiguára warrior is like the Ostrich[3] which flies along the earth; we will follow him like his wings," said Iraçéma.

The Chief shook his head anew.

"Whilst the Sea-Warrior slept the enemy ran. Those who first set out are now near, as the horns are to the bow."

Shame gnawed the heart of Martim.

"Let the Chief Poty fly and save Iraçéma. The bad warrior, who would not listen to the voice of his brother and the wish of his bride, can only die."

Martim began to retrace his steps.

"The soul of the white warrior does not listen to

---

[1] *Zabelê*, a small bird somewhat like a partridge.
[2] *Tapyr*, a well-known animal about the size of a calf. The hide is useful, and of buff colour. It is also called *Tapijeretê*, *Tapy'ra*, and *Tapy'ra caapóra*.
[3] In the original *Ema*, the South American ostrich.

his mouth. Poty and his brother have but one life."

The lip of Iraçéma spoke not—only smiled.

———

CHAPTER XVIII.

THE forest literally trembled as it echoed the career of the Tabajára braves.

The form of Irapúam the Great first looms amidst the trees. His suffused eye caught sight of the white warrior through a cloud of blood ; a hoarse and tiger-like roar burst from his brawny chest.

The Tabajára Chief and his tribe were about to fall upon the fugitives like the swollen waves which break on the Mocoribe's [1] flank.

But hush !—in the distance sounds the bark of the Indian dog.

Poty gave a cry of joy.

" It is Poty's hound that guides the warriors of his Taba to save his brother."

The hoarse sea-shell of the Pytiguáras bellowed through the forest. The great Jacaúna, Lord of the Sea-shores, was marching from the river of the herons with the best of his braves.

The Pytiguáras receive the first assault of the foe on the jagged heads of their shafts, which they loosed in showers like the porcupine [2] raising his quills. Presently resounded the War-Poçema of the Taba-járas ; the space between the enemies was narrowed, and the hand-to-hand combat began.

Jacaúna attacked Irapúam. The horrible fight

---

[1] *Mocoribe*, now called *Mucuripe*, means " to make glad ; " it is a hill of sand in a bay of the same name, a league from Fortaleza, the great seaport town of Ceará.

[2] In the original *Coandú*, porcupine.

was that of ten braves, yet it did not exhaust the strength of the two great chiefs. When their toma-hawks clashed, the battle trembled to the heart as one man.

The brother of Iraçéma came straight to the stranger who had taken the daughter of Araken from the hospitable Wigwam ; the trail of vengeance led him ; the sight of his sister maddened him. Cauby the brave furiously assaults the enemy.

Iraçéma remained by the side of her warrior and spouse. She saw Cauby from afar and cried—

" Let the Lord of Iraçéma listen to the prayer of his slave ; let him not shed the blood of the son of Araken. If the warrior Cauby must die, let it be by the hand of Iraçéma, not by his."

Martim looked at the savage with eyes of horror.

" Would Iraçéma slay her brother ? "

" Iraçéma would see the blood of Cauby stain her hand rather than the hand of her lord, because the eyes of Iraçéma dwell upon him, and not upon herself."

The battle still rages. Cauby fights with fury. The Christian hardly defends himself, but the poisoned arrows from the young wife's bow save him from the blows of the enemy.

Poty had already laid low the old Andira and all the braves who during the struggle had encountered his good tomahawk. Martim leaves to him the son of Araken and seeks out Irapúam.

" Jacaúna is a great Chief ; his War-collar,[1] thrice encircles his neck ! This Tabájara belongs to the white warrior."

" Revenge is the honour of warfare, and Jacaúna loves the friend of Poty."

The great Pytiguára chief upraised his formidable

---

[1] *Seu collar de guerra.* The collar which the savages made of the teeth of vanquished enemies (taking from each one tooth), was a blazon and a proof of valour.

tomahawk. The duel between Irapúam and Martim began. The Christian's sword was shivered by the savage's tomahawk. The Tabajára Chief advanced upon his unarmed adversary.

Iraçéma hissed like the Boicininga,[1] and threw herself between her warrior and the Tabajára; at once the massive weapon trembled in his powerful right hand and his arm fell inanimate by his side.

The Poçema of victory sounded. The Pytiguára warriors, headed by Jacaúna and Poty, swept the forest. The Tabajáras snatched, as they fled, their Chief from the hatred and vengeance of the daughter of Araken, who had the power of conquering him, as the Jandáia prostrates the tallest and strongest palm-tree by nibbling the core.

The eyes of Iraçéma, scanning the forest, saw the ground strewed with the bodies of her brethren, and in the distance the remnant of their war-party flying in a black cloud of dust. That blood which stained the ground was the same brave blood which now lit up her cheeks with shame.

The grief-drops moistened her beautiful cheek. Martim withdrew that he might not embarrass her sorrow. He wished her naked woe to bathe itself in tear floods.

CHAPTER XIX.

Poty returned from pursuing the foe. His eyes filled with delight when he saw the white warrior safe.

The faithful dog followed him closely, still licking from its hairy mouth the Tabajára blood, of which it had drunk its fill. Its master caressed it, pleased by its courage and devotion. It had saved Martim by guiding so diligently the warriors of Jacaúna.

[1] A large species of boa.

"The bad spirits of the forest may again separate the white warrior from his Pytiguára brother. The dog will henceforth follow him, so that even from a distance Poty may hear his call."

"But the dog is thy companion and faithful friend."

"It will be Poty's companion and friend still more when it serves his brother than when it serves him. The white warrior shall call it 'Japy,'[1] and it will be the fleet foot with which from afar they will run to each other."

Jacaúna gave the signal of departure.

The Pytiguára warriors marched for the glad banks of the Heron's River, where rose the great Taba of the Prairie Lords.

The sun declined and again soared in the heavens. The warriors arrived where the sea-range fell towards the midlands. Already they had passed that part of the mountain which, being scant of tree and shorn like the Capivára,[2] the people of Tupan had called Ibyapina.[3]

Poty took the Christian where grew a leafy Jatobá,[4] that overtopped the trees of the Serra's highest point when waving before the wind; it seemed to sweep the sky with its immense dome.

"On this spot the white warrior's brother was born," said the Pytiguára Chief.

Martim embraced the enormous trunk.

---

[1] *Japy* means "our foot."

[2] *Capivára, capiuára* (that which lives on Capim, the coarse grass of the country), is a kind of water-hog. The Peruvian people of Rio Branco wear the teeth of this animal as earrings.

[3] *Ibyapina* means "bald land."

[4] *Jatobá*, an enormous and royal-looking tree. The place where this scene took place is now called Villa Viçosa, where tradition says Poty, afterwards Camarão, was born. Jatobá is the name of a river and of a Serra in South Quiteria, and Jatobá was the name of the father of Poty and Jacaúna.

"Jatobá, thou that sawest my brother Poty come into the world : the stranger embraces thee ! "

" May the lightning wither thee, O tree of the warrior Poty ! when his brother abandons him."

Then the chief spoke as follows :—

"Then Jacaúna was not yet a warrior. Jatobá, our greatest Chief, was leading the Pytiguáras to victory. As soon as the full waters began to run, he marched straight for the Serra. Arriving here, he sent for the whole Taba, that it might be nearer the enemy, to vanquish them again. The same moon which saw their arrival shone upon the hammock in which Sahy, his wife, gave him one more warrior of his blood. The moonlight played amongst the leafage of the Jatobá, and the smile upon the lips of the great and wise Chief who had taken its name and might."

Iraçema approached.

The turtle-dove,[1] feeding in the sands, leaves its mate, who flits restlessly from branch to branch, and coos that the absent one may reply. Thus the forest girl wandered in search of her prop, softly humming a gentle, tender song.

Martim received her with his soul in his eyes, and leading his wife on the side of his heart, and his friend on the side of his strength, returned to the Ranch[2] of the Pytiguáras.

CHAPTER XX.

THE moon waxed rounder. Three suns had passed since Martim and Iraçema had been in the lands of the Pytiguáras, Lords of the banks of the rivers

---

[1] In the original *Rôla*.
[2] *Rancho* is a shed made of mud and sticks, and thatched with Sapé leaves or roofed with tiles.

Camocim and Acaráu.[1] The strangers had hung their hammocks in the large cabin of the great Jacaúna. The brave Chief claimed for himself the pleasure of being the white warrior's host.

Poty abandoned his wigwam that he might accompany his brother of war to the cabin of his brother by blood, and to enjoy every moment that the sea-warrior could spare to devote to friendship from the love of Iraçéma.

Darkness had already left the face of the earth, but Martim saw that it had not left the face of his wife since the day of the combat.

" Sorrow lives in the soul of Iraçéma ! "

" The wife's gladness can come only from her husband. When thy eyes leave Iraçéma's, tears fill them."

" Why weeps the daughter of the Tabajáras ? "

"This is the Taba of the Pytiguáras, enemies of her people. The sight of Iraçéma still sees the skulls of her brothers staked round the Caiçára, her ears still listen to the death-song of the Tabajára captives, her hand still touches arms dyed with the blood of her fathers."

The bride placed her two hands on the warrior's shoulders and reclined upon his breast.

" Iraçéma will suffer all for her warrior and lord. The Atá fruit [2] is sweet and pleasant, but when bruised it sours. Thy wife would not that her love sour thy heart. She would fill it with the sweetness of honey."

" Let calm return to the breast of the daughter of the Tabajáras. She shall leave the Taba of her people's foes."

The Christian marched straight to the cabin of Jacaúna. The Great Chief was joyful on seeing his

[1] Two rivers of Ceará, discharging into the ocean.
[2] The *Atá*, custard-apple.

guest arrive, but joy soon fled from his warlike brow when Martim said—

"The white warrior is going to leave thy cabin, Great Chief."

"Then there is something wanting to him in the cabin of Jacaúna?"

"Thy guest hath wanted nothing. He was happy here; but the voice of his heart sends him to another place."

"Then leave, and take all that is needful for the journey. May Tupan fortify my brother, and bring him back again to the cabin of Jacaúna, that he may celebrate his wellcoming."

Poty arrived: hearing that the sea-warrior was going, he said—

"Thy brother will accompany thee."

"Will not Poty's warriors need their chief?"

"Unless my brother desires that they go with Poty, Jacaúna will lead them to victory."

"The cabin of Poty will be deserted and sad."

"The heart of the white brave's brother would be still more desert and sad without him."

The sea-warrior left the banks of the River of the Herons, and marched towards the land where the sun sets. His wife and friend followed his steps. They went beyond the fertile forest range, where the abundant fruits breed a swarm of flies, from which it takes the name of Meruoca.[1]

They crossed the little streams which discharge their waters into the River of the Herons, and they sighted on the far horizon a high mountain-range. The day expired; a black cloud seemed to be advancing from the sea. It was the Urubús,[2] that feast on the dead which the ocean throws up on the beach, and return with the night to their nests.

[1] *Meru-oca* means "the Fly's House." It is a Serra close to Sobral, fertile in all that is useful as food.

[2] *Urubú*, the Brazilian turkey-buzzard.

The travellers slept at Uruburetama.[1] When the sun reappeared, it found them on the banks of the river which rises in the Serra-gap, and descends winding like a serpent into the plain. Its mazes deceive, at every step, the pilgrims who follow its tortuous course ; for which reason it was called the Mundahú.[2]

Following its cool banks, Martim, on the second sun, beheld the green seas and the white beaches, where the murmuring waves now sob, and then, raging with fury, break in flakes of foam.

The eyes of the white warrior dilated at the vast expanse, his chest heaved. This same sea also kissed the white sands of the Potengi,[3] his cradle, where he first saw the light of America. He threw himself into the waves, and revelled in the thought that he bathed his body in the waters of his native country, and his soul in yearning for it.

Iraçéma felt her heart weep, but soon her warrior's smile reassured her.

Meantime Poty from the top of a palm tree arrowed the savoury Camoropim,[4] which sported in the little bay of Mundahú, and prepared the Moquem for their refection.

CHAPTER XXI.

THE sun had already left the zenith. The travellers reach the mouth of that river where the savoury Tra-

[1] *Uruburetama*, a high mountain-range which swarms with vultures' nests.

[2] *Mundahú*, a tortuous river rising in the Serra of Uruburetama ; from *mundé*, a snare, and *hú* or *ú a* river.

[3] *Potengi*, the river that waters the city of Natal, a seaport town of Rio Grande do Norte, where Martim Soares Moreno was born.

[4] *Camoropim*, a large fish, tasting like a codfish.

hira [1] salmon breeds abundantly, and whose banks are peopled by fishermen of the great Pytiguára race.

They received the strangers with that generous hospitality which was a law of their religion, and Poty with the respect due to so great a warrior, and to a brother of Jacaúna, the most powerful Chief of the Pytiguáras.

To rest the travellers, and to dismiss them with proper ceremony, the Chief of the Tribe received Martim, Iraçéma, and Poty in the Jangada, and spreading a sail to the breeze, bore them far down the coast. All the fishermen in their rafts followed their Chief, and filled the air with a song of lament, accompanied by the murmurings of the Uraça,[2] which imitates the sobbing of the wind.

Beyond the fishing tribe, and nearer the Serras, was the hunting tribe. They occupied the borders of the Soipé,[3] covered with forests, where abounded deer, the fat Paca, and the slender Jacu.[4] Hence the dwellers of these regions had named it the Hunting-Ground.

Jaguarassú, or Great Tiger, the Chief of these hunters, had a Wigwam on the banks of the lake formed by the river as it nears the sea. Here the travellers met with the same warm reception which they had received from the fishermen.

After leaving Soipé, the travellers crossed the river

---

[1] *As saborosas trahiras.* The river Trahiry, from *trahira*, name of a savage fish, and *oy* water or river, is thirty leagues north of the capital of Ceará.

[2] *Uraça*, a sort of flute which they made of big shells.

[3] *Soipé*, hunting-ground, from *soo*, "game," and *ipé*, "the place where." Now it is called Siupé, and its river and village belong to the parish and township of Fortaleza. It is situated on the banks of marshes called Jaguarassú, at the mouth of the river.

[4] *Jacu* (*Crax Penelope*), a large bird, of which there are four different kinds; it tastes and looks, when cooked, somewhat like, but much better than, our pheasant.

Pacoty,[1] on whose borders flourished the leafy banana, waving its green plumes.

Farther on is the Iguápe[2] stream, whose waters encircle the dunes of sand.

In the distance, crowning the horizon, appeared a high sand-hill, snowy white as the ocean foam. The summit overhung the palms and cocos, and appeared like the bald head of the Condor,[3] there awaiting the storm blowing up from the ocean bounds.

" Poty knows the great hill of sand?" asked the Christian.

" Poty knows all the land that belongs to the Pytiguáras, from the banks of the great river which forms an arm of the sea,[4] to the banks of the stream where the Jaguar lives. He has been already to the height of Mocoribe, and thence he has seen, far at sea, the big Igáras[5] of the white warriors, the enemies of my brother, who dwell in Mearim."

" Why callest thou the great sand-hill Mocoribe?"

" The fisherman of the beach, who puts out to sea in Jangádas, there where the Aty[6] flies, is sad because he is far from his cabin where sleep the children of his blood. When he returns, and his eyes first behold the hill of sand, gladness returns to the man's breath. Then he says that the hill of the sands gives joy."

[1] *Pacoty*, river of the Pacobas. It rises in the Serra of Baturité, and empties itself into the ocean, two leagues north of Aquirás. *Pacoba*, also called *Pacoeira* and *Musa*, is the indigenous banana of Brazil, a shrubby growth some ten or twelve feet high, and as thick as a man's thigh, yet so soft that it may be cut down with a single stroke of the sword.

[2] *Iguápe*, a bay distant two miles from Aquirás. The word, which is common in Brazil, means "water which encircles."

[3] The well-known and monstrous bird of the eagle species, with a very hard, sharp beak that will pierce a bull's hide.

[4] *Rio que forma um braço do mar.* This is the Parnahyba, the main river of Piauhy, and literally means "arm running from the sea."

[5] *Igáras*, big canoes, meaning the ships of the French.

[6] *Aty*, seagull.

" The fisherman says well ; thy brother, like him, is happy when he sees the mountain of sand."

Martim and Poty ascended the head of Mocoribe. Iraçéma followed, with her eyes, her spouse, wandering like the Jaçanan [1] round the beautiful bay, which earth formed to receive the sea. On her way she collected the sweet Cajús, which appease the warriors' thirst, and gathered delicate shells to ornament her neck.

The travellers dwelt in Mocoribe three suns. Then Martim directed his steps beyond it. The wife and friend followed him to the bank of a river, whose banks were overflowed and covered with mangrove. The sea entering into it formed a basin of clear crystalline water, which appeared almost scooped out of the stone like a vase of pottery.

Whilst reconnoitring this place the Christian warrior began to reflect. To the present time he had marched without any object, and he had allowed his steps to guide him where they would. He had no other thought except to absent himself from the Taba of the Pytiguáras, that he might the better soothe the sorrow in Iraçéma's heart. The Christian knew by experience that travel cures a Saudade, because the soul rests whilst the body moves. But now seated on the beach he pondered.

Poty came.

" The white warrior thinks ; the breast of his brother is open to receive his thought."

" Poty's brother thinks that this is a better place than the margins of Jaguaribe for the Taba of the warriors of his race. In these waters the big Igáras that come from the far-off land may lie sheltered from wind and sea : hence they can fall upon Mearim and destroy

[1] *Jaçanan*, a bird called in Africa a lily-trotter : here a waterhen, scarlet and green.

the white Tapuios,[1] the allies of the Tabajáras, enemies of Poty's nation."

The Pytiguára chief reflected and replied—

" My brother may go and bring his warriors. Poty will plant his Taba close to the Mayry[2] of his friend."

Iraçéma drew nigh. The Christian made a gesture of silence to the Pytiguára chief.

" The voice of the husband is silent, and his eyes fall when Iraçéma comes. Shall she depart ? "

" Thy husband wants thee nearer, that his voice and eyes may penetrate still deeper into thy soul."

The beautiful savage was radiant with smiles, as the ripening flower opens its petals, and she leant upon the shoulder of her warrior.

" Iraçéma listens to thee."

" These plains are joyful, and will be more so when Iraçéma dwells in them. What says her heart ? "

" Iraçéma's heart is ever glad when she is with her lord and warrior."

The Christian followed the bank of the river and chose a place for his Wigwam. Poty felled the Carnaúba to make props of its trunks ; the daughter of Araken weaved, fanlike, the fronds of the palms to thatch the roof and cloth the walls. Martim dug the trenches, and made a door of laths and layers of bamboo.

When night came, the lovers slung their hammock in their new cabin, and the friend slept in the porch which faced the rising sun.|

[1] *Brancos tapuios ;* in Tupy, *Tapuitininga.* A name the Pytiguáras gave to the French, to distinguish them from Tupinambás. The word means the " Deserters of their village."

[2] *Mayry*, city, comes from *mayr*, stranger, and was applied to the settlements of the whites to distinguish them from the Indian villages ; in fact, a strangery.

CHAPTER XXII.

Poty saluted his friend and spoke as follows :—

"Ere the father of Jacaúna and Poty, the valiant warrior Jatobá, ruled over all the Pytiguára warriors, the Great Tomahawk of the Nation was in the right hand of Batuireté,[1] the Head Chief, Sire of Jatobá. It was he who came along the sea-beach to the river of the Jaguars, and expelled the Tabajáras into the interior, and dictated to each tribe the limits of its lands. Then he entered the inner regions as far as the Serra which takes his name.

"When his stars were many,[2] so many that his Camocim no longer contained all the nuts that mark the number of his years, his body began to incline earthwards, his arm stiffened like the branch of the unbending Ubiratan, and his eyes grew dark. He then called the warrior Jatobá and said, 'Let my son take the Tomahawk of the Pytiguára Nation. Tupan wills not that Batuireté should carry it any more to war, since he has taken from him the strength of his body, the use of his arm, and the light of his eyes. But Tupan has been good to him, since he gave him a son like the warrior Jatobá."

"Jatobá took the Tomahawk of the Pytiguáras. Batuireté assumed the staff of his old age and set out. He crossed the vast uninhabited regions to the luxuriant prairies, where run the waters that come from the quarter of the night. As the old warrior dragged his limbs along their banks, and the light of his eyes would not let him behold nor the fruits, nor

[1] *Batuireté*, "celebrated snipe." The soubriquet of this great Chief signifies that he was a "brave swimmer." It is also the name of a very fertile Serra, and the region which he occupied.

[2] *Suas estrellas erão muitas.* The savages counted their years by the heliacal rising of the Pleiades, and also by keeping a cashew-nut of each spring.

the trees, nor the birds of the air, he said in his sadness, 'Ah! my bygone days!'"

"The people who heard him wept over the ruins of the Great Chief; and since then, whoever passes by that spot repeats his words, 'Ah! meus tempos passados;' for which reason the river and the prairie are called Quixeramobim.[1]

"Batuireté came from the 'Path of the Herons'[2] as far as that Serra which thou seest in the distance, and there he first lived. On the topmost peak the old warrior made his nest, as high as flies the hawk, to pass the remnant of his days speaking with Tupan. His son already sleeps under the earth, whilst he, even during the last moon, was thinking at his cabin door, to await the night which brings the Great Sleep. All the Pytiguára warriors, when the voice of war awakes them, visit and beg the old man that he will teach them to conquer; for no other warrior ever knew to fight as he did. Thus the tribes call him no more by his name, but know him as the Great Wise Man of War—Maranguab.[3]

"The chief Poty wants to visit the Serra to see his mighty Grandsire; but before day falls he will be back in the cabin of his brother. Has he any other wish?"

"The white warrior will accompany his brother. He wants to embrace the Great Chief of the Pytiguáras, Grandfather of Poty, and to tell the old man that he lives again in his grandson."

Martim called Iraçéma, and they both set out,

---

[1] *Quixeramobim*, translated into Portuguese, means, "Ah! meus outros tempos;" in English, "Ah! my other times."

[2] *Caminho dos garças*, or flight of the herons, in Tupy is *Acarapé*, a village in the parish of Batuireté, nine leagues from the capital of Ceará.

[3] *Maranguab* means "to war" and "wise man." Maranguape, five leagues' distant from the capital, is noted for its beauty and fertility.

guided by the Pytiguára, to the Serra of Maranguab,
which loomed above the horizon. They followed the
course of the river to the place where it is joined by
the stream of Pirapora.[1]

The cabin of the old warrior was close to one of
those beautiful cascades where the fish leap in the
midst of the bubbling foam. The waters here are
fresh and sweet, like the sea-breeze in the hour of
heat, murmuring amongst the palm-leaves.

Batuireté was sitting upon one of the cascade rocks;
the burning sun-rays fell full upon his head, which
was bald and wrinkled as the Genipapo.[2] Thus
sleeps the Jaburú[3] at the edge of the tank.

"Poty has arrived at the cabin of the great Maranguab, father of Jatobá, and has brought his white
brother to see the greatest Warrior of the Nations."

The old man only opened his heavy eyelids, and
passed a long but feeble look from the grandson to
the stranger. Then his chest heaved and his lips
murmured—

"Tupan wills that these eyes should see, before
being quenched, the White Hawk side by side with
the Narseja."[4]

The Abaeté dropped his head on his chest, and
spoke no more, nor moved again.

Poty and Martim, supposing that he slept, respect-
fully withdrew, not to disturb the repose of one who

[1] *Pirapora*, a river of Maranguape, noted for the freshness of
its waters and the excellence of its baths. They are in the
environs of the Cachoeiras (rapids, cataracts, or waterfalls),
and are called the "Baths of Pirapora." The word means
"fish-leap."

[2] *Genipapo*, a well-known Brazilian tree, whose fruit produces
a dark dye with which the Indians used to tattoo themselves.

[3] *Jaburú*, a large crane.

[4] *O gavião branco*, the white hawk, whilst *Narseja* is the snipe.
Batuireté thus calling the stranger, and speaking of his grandson
as a snipe by comparison, prophesied the destruction of his race
by the whites. It was the last word he spoke.

had done such deeds during his long life. Iraçéma, who had bathed in the nearest Cachoeira, came to meet them, bringing combs of the purest honey in a leaf of the Taioba.[1]

The friends wandered about the flourishing environs till the shade of the mountain darkened the valley. They then returned to the spot where they had left the Maranguab.

The old man was still there in the same attitude, with his head bent on his chest and his crossed knees supporting his forehead. The ants were running up his body, and the Tuins[2] were fluttering around him and settling upon his bald head.

Poty placed his hand on the old man's head, and felt that he was dead. He had died of old age.

The Pytiguára Chief then intoned the Song of Death; presently he went into the cabin to fetch the Camoçim, which was filled to overflowing with nuts of Cajú. Martim counted five times five handfuls.

Meanwhile, Iraçéma gathered in the forest the Andiroba,[3] with which to anoint the body of the old man in the Camoçim, where the dutiful hand of his grandson placed him. The Funeral Vase remained suspended to the cabin roof.

They then planted the Ortiga, or large stinging nettle, before the doorway, to defend against animals the abandoned Oca.[4] Poty bade a sorrowful farewell to these scenes, and returned with his companions to the borders of the sea.

---

[1] *Taioba*, a bush with large leaves, from *ca*, tree, and *oba*, dress, clothing.
[2] *Tuins* in Brazil is a kind of little parrot.
[3] *Andiroba*, a large tree, native of Brazil, which is of an aromatic nature, and gives a bitter oil.
[4] *Oca*, house, cabin, wigwam.

CHAPTER XXIII.

FOUR moons had lighted the heavens since Iraçéma had left the plains of Ipú, and three since she had dwelt in the Wigwam of her husband by the shore of the sea.

Gladness dwelt within her soul. The daughter of the forest was happy as the swallow that abandons its paternal nest and goes forth to build a new home in the land where the flower-season begins. Iraçéma likewise found there, on the sea-shore, a nest of love —the heart's new country!

She wandered over the beautiful plains like the humming-bird hovering amongst the flowers of the acacia. The light of early morning found her already clinging to the shoulder of her husband, ever smiling, like the Enrediça,[1] which twines round the tree-trunk, and which covers it with a new garland every morning.

Martim went out to hunt with Poty. He then separated himself from her in order to have the pleasure of returning to her.

In the middle of a green pasture hard by was a beautiful lake, to which the wild girl used to direct her light step. It was the hour of the morning bath. She would cast herself into the water, and swim with the white herons and the scarlet Jaçanans. The Pytiguára warriors who chanced to come that way called this the "Lake of Beauty," because it was bathed in by Iraçéma, the most beautiful of the race of Tupan.

And from that time till now, mothers come from afar to dip their daughters in the waters of the Por-

---

[1] *Enrediça,* a creeper which entwines and entangles round a tree-trunk.

angába,[1] which they suppose have the virtue of making the virgins beautiful and beloved by the braves.

After the bath Iraçéma wandered to the skirts of the Serra of Maranguab, where rises the river of the Marrecas.[2] There in the cool shade grew the most savoury fruits of the country; she would collect a plentiful supply, and rock herself in the branches of the Maracujá-tree, waiting for Martim to return from hunting.

Her fancy did not always, however, lead her to the Jerarahú,[3] but often to the opposite side, close to the lake of the Sapiranga,[4] whose waters are said to inflame the eyes. Near it was a wood, thick and leafy, with clumps of Muritys, which formed in the middle of the plateau a large island of beautiful palms. Iraçéma loved the Murityapúa,[5] where the wind blew softly. Here she stripped the pulp from the red Coco to make refreshing drinks, mixed with the bee-honey, which the warriors liked to drink in the great heat of the day.

One morning Poty guided Martim to the chase. They marched towards a Serra which towers on the opposite side to Maranguab, its twin sister. The highest peak bends like the hooked beak of the macaw, and hence the warriors named it Aratanha.[6]

---

[1] *Porangaba* means beauty; it is a lake in a delightful spot, distant one league from the City. Now it is called Arronches; on its banks is a decayed village of the same name.

[2] *Marrecas*, wild ducks.

[3] *Jerarahú*, "river of the wild ducks." This place is even now notable for its delicious fruits, especially the beautiful oranges known as the oranges of Jerarahú.

[4] *Sapiranga*, which means "red eyes," and they also call by this name a certain ophthalmia in the North. It is a lake close to Alagadiço Novo, about two leagues from the Capital.

[5] *Murityapúa*, where there is now a small town. The word is from *murity*, palm, and *apúam*, an island or clump.

[6] *Aratanha*, from *arara*, a macaw, and *tanha*, teeth. A fertile and cultivated Serra, which is a continuation of Maranguape.

They mounted by the side of Guaiuba,[1] whence the waters descend into the valley, and they went to the stream where the Pacas are to be found.

The sun shone on the Macaw's Beak only when the hunters descended from Pacatuba[2] to the plateau. From afar they saw Iraçéma, who came to wait for them on the margin of her lake, the Porangába. She came towards them with the proud step of the heron stalking by the water's edge. Outside her Carioba she wore a belt of Maniva, the flowers of which are an emblem of fruitfulness. A festoon of the same flowers twined round her throat and fell over her marble bosom.

She seized the hand of her husband and carried it to her lips.

"Thy blood lives in the bosom of Iraçéma. She will be the mother of thy son."

"*Son* saidst thou?" exclaimed the Christian with joy.

Kneeling down, he threw his arm around her and kissed her, mutely thanking God for this great happiness.

When he arose Poty spoke—

"The happiness of the young brave is a wife and a friend; the first gives gladness, the second gives strength. The warrior without a spouse is like a tree lacking leaves and flowers; never shall he behold its fruit. The brave without a friend is like the solitary tree waving in the midst of the prairie with each blast of wind; its fruit never ripens. The happiness of the strong man is the offspring which is born to him, and which is his pride. Every warrior of his blood is one branch more to raise up his name to the sky, like the

---

[1] *Guaiuba*, which means "whence come the waters of the valley," is a river rising in the Serra of Aratanha, and crossing the village of the same name, six leagues from the capital.

[2] *Pacatuba*, "bed of the Pacas." There is now a new but important village in a beautiful valley of the Serra of Aratanha.

top branch of the cedar. Beloved by Tupan is the warrior who has a wife, a friend, and many sons. He has nothing more to desire save a glorious death."

Martim pressed his bosom to that of Poty.

"The heart of both husband and friend speaks by the mouth of Poty. The white warrior is blest, O Chief of the Pytiguáras, Lords of the Sea-shores; and happiness was born to him in the Land of the Palm-trees, where the Baúnilha perfumes the air; it was begotten by the blood of thy race, who bear on their faces the colour of the sun's ray. The white warrior no longer desires any other country save the land of his son and of his heart."

At the break of dawn Poty set out to gather the seeds of the Crajurú,[1] which yields a most beautiful red dye, and the bark of the Angico, whence is extracted a lustrous black. On the way his unerring arrow brought down a wild duck sailing in the air, and he took from its wings the longest feathers. He then ascended Mocoribe and sounded the Inubia. The sea-breeze carried far the hoarse sound. The Shell of the Fishermen of the Trahiry and the Horn of the Hunters of the Soipé gave answer.

Martim bathed in the river waters, and walked on the beach to dry himself in the wind and sun. By his side ran Iraçéma, collecting the yellow ambergris[2] cast up by the sea. Every night the wife perfumed her body and the white hammock, that the love of the warrior might remain captivated.

Poty returned.

---

[1] *Crajurú,* a tree whose seeds give a scarlet dye.
[2] *Ambar.* The sea-beach of Ceará was at that time full of ambergris, cast up by the sea. The savages call it *Pirarepoti,* "the secretion of a fish."

CHAPTER XXIV.

IT was customary amongst the race of Tupan for the brave to wear on his body the colours of his nation. They first traced upon the skin black lines like those of the Coaty,[1] whence came the name of the War-painting art. They also varied the colours, and many warriors were covered with emblems of their deeds.

The stranger having adopted the country of his spouse and his friend, was expected to pass through this ceremony in order to become a redskin warrior and a son of Tupan. With this intention Poty had provided for himself the necessary objects.

Iraçéma prepared the dyes, the Chief dipping in them the feathers, traced over the warrior's body the red and black lines, the Pytiguára colours. He then drew on his forehead an arrow, and said—

"As the arrow pierces the hard trunk, so the warrior's eye penetrates the soul of the people."

On the arm a hawk.

"As the Anajê swoops from the clouds, so falls the warrior's arm upon the enemy."

On the left foot the root of a palm tree.

"As the little root supports in the ground the lofty palm tree, thus the firm foot of the warrior sustains his frame."

On the right foot a wing.

"As the wing of the Majoy[2] cleaves the air, thus the fleet foot of the warrior has no equal in the race."

---

[1] *Coaty*, a small fox-like animal, a racoon, whose hide has a red ground with black stripes. *Coatyara*, he who paints ; *coatyá*, to paint ; *coatyabo*, he who is painted. History mentions the fact that Martim Soares Moreno painted and dressed like the savages of Ceará whilst he was living amongst them.

[2] *Majoy*, swallow.

Iraçéma then took the feather-vane, and painted a leaf with a bee upon it : her voice murmured through her smiles—

" As the bee makes honey in the black heart of the Jacarandá, so sweetness is in the breast of the bravest warrior."

Martim opened his arms and lips to receive the body and soul of his wife.

" My brother is a great warrior of the Pytiguára nation. He wants a name in the language of his new country."

" The name of thy brother shall be called by whatever part of his body thou imposest thy hand upon."

" Coatyábo ! " exclaimed Iraçéma.

" Thou hast said it. I am the painted warrior, the warrior of the wife and of the friend."

Poty gave to his brother the bow and the tomahawk, which were the noble arms of a brave. Iraçéma had prepared for him the plumes and ornamented belt worn by illustrious Chiefs.

The daughter of Araken fetched from the cabin the meats of the feast and the wines of the Genipapo and Mandioca. The warriors drank copiously and danced joyous dances. Whilst they revolved round the bonfires they sang songs of gladness.

Poty chanted.

" As the Cobra-Snake which has two heads and only one body, so is the friendship of Coatyábo and Poty."

Iraçéma took up the refrain.

" As the oyster which leaves not the rock until after death, so is Iraçéma joined to her husband."

The warriors chanted.

" As the Jatobá in the forest, so is the warrior Coatyábo between his brother and spouse ; his branches entwine with those of the Ubiratan, and his shade protects the humble grass."

The fires of joy burnt until morning came, and with them lasted the Feast of the Warriors.

CHAPTER XXV.

Joy still reigned in the cabin during the whole time whilst the ears of corn ripened and waxed yellow.

Once at break of day the Christian was strolling by the borders of the sea. His soul was weary.

The humming-bird satiates itself with honey and perfume; it then sleeps in its little white nest of cotton, until another year comes round with its Moon of Flowers. Like it, the warrior's soul is sated with happiness; it wants sleep and repose.

Hunting and excursions in the mountains with his friend by his side, the tender caresses of the wife awaiting his return, the pleasant Carbeto[1] in the Wigwam porch, no longer awakened in him emotions as they were wont to do. His heart began to speak.

Iraçéma was sporting on the beach. His eyes wandered from her over the sea's vast expanse.

Large white wings were seen hovering over the blue waste. The Christian knew that it was a big Igára of many sails, such as were constructed by his brethren, and the Saudade of his country wrung his breast.

High rose the sun; the warrior on the shore followed with his eyes the white wings as they fled. In vain the wife called him to the hut, in vain she displayed to his eyes her graces, or offered him the best fruits of the country. The warrior never moved until the sail disappeared behind the horizon.

Poty returned from the Serra, where for the first time he had been alone. He had left serenity on his brother's countenance, and now he found there sorrow. Martim went forth to meet him.

"The great Igára of the white Tapúia is on the sea. The eyes of Poty's brother saw them flying

---

[1] *Carbe'o*, a sort of evening meeting of the Indians in a large cabin where they used to converse.

towards the banks of the Mearim. They are the allies of the Tupinambás[1] and the enemies of his and my race."

"Poty is lord of a thousand bows; if Coatyabo wishes, he will accompany him with his braves to the banks of the Mearim to conquer the Tapúitinga, and his friends the treacherous Tupinambás."

"When it is time, Poty's brother will tell him."

The warriors returned to the cabin where Iraçéma was. The sweet song to-day was silent on the wife's lips. She wove amidst her sighs the fringe of the maternal hammock, broader and thicker than the marriage-cot. Poty, who saw her thus occupied, spoke.

"When the Sabiá sings, it is the season of love. When, silent, it makes the nest for the little one: it is the time for work."

"My brother speaks like the Ran[2] announcing the rain, but the Sabiá which makes its nest does not know if it will sleep in it."

The voice of Iraçéma trembled. Her eye sought Martim. He was thinking. The words of Iraçéma passed over him like the breeze upon the smooth surface of the rocks, noiseless and echoless.

The sun still shone on the sea-beach, and the sands reflected its ardent rays, but neither the light which came from heaven nor that which earth gave could drive darkness from the Christian's soul. Every moment the twilight deepened on his forehead.

Arrived from the banks of the Acaraú a Pytiguára warrior, sent by Jacaúna to his brother Poty. He had followed the warriors' trail as far as the Trahiry, whence the Fishermen had guided him to the Wigwam.

---

[1] *Tupinambás* means fathers of the Tupys, a formidable nation, the primitive branch of the great Tupy race. After an heroic resistance, not being able to expel the Portuguese from Bahia, they migrated to Maranhão, where they formed alliance with the French, who overran these regions.

[2] *Ran*, frog.

Poty was alone in the porch. He rose up and bent his head, to listen with more gravity and respect to the words which his brother had sent him by the mouth of the messenger.

"The Tapuitinga who was in the Mearim came through the forests as far as the beginning of the Ibyapába, where he had made an alliance with Irapúam to fight the Pytiguára nation. They are coming down the Serra to the banks of the river where the herons drink, and where Poty raised the Tabá of his warriors. Jacaúna now summons him to defend the lands of our fathers, and his people want their greatest warrior."

"The warrior must return to the banks of Acaraú, and his foot must not rest until it has trodden the floor of Jacaúna's Wigwam. When he arrives, he will say to the great chief, '*Jacaúna's brother has arrived at the Taba of his warriors*'—and he will not lie."

The messenger departed.

Poty aroused himself, and walked towards the plains, guided by the trail of Coatyabo. He met him far beyond, wandering amongst the reeds and rushes which border the banks of Jacaratuy.[1]

"The white Tapuia is in the Ibyapába, to help the Tabajáras against Jacaúna. Poty is hastening to defend the land of his brothers, and the Taba where sleep the Camocins of his fathers. He will know how to conquer quickly, in order to return to Coatyábo."

"Poty's brother goes with him. Nothing separates two warrior-friends when sounds the Inubia of war."

"My brother is great like the sea, and good like the sky."

The two friends embraced, and marched with their faces turned to the quarter of the rising sun.

---

[1] *Jacaratuy*, a lake near the present town of Ceará.

CHAPTER XXVI.

WALKING—ever walking—the braves arrived at the borders of a lake which was in the plateau-land.

The Christian suddenly stopped and turned his face towards the sea. The sadness left his heart and rose to his forehead.

" My brother's foot has taken root in the Land of Love," said the Chief. " Let him remain. Poty will quickly return."

" Poty's brother will accompany him. He has said it, and his word is like the arrow of Poty's bow; when it whistles, it has already pierced the mark."

" Does my brother then wish that Iraçéma should accompany him to the banks of the Acaraú ? "

" We go to fight her brothers. The Taba of the Pytiguáras would only be to her a scene of pain and sadness. The daughter of the Tabajáras should remain."

" What then does Coatyábo await ? "

" Poty's brother is afflicted because the daughter of the Tabajáras may be sad, and abandon the Wigwam without awaiting his return. Before departing, he would wish to soothe the spirit of the wife."

Poty took thought.

" The tears of Woman soften the warrior's heart as the morning dew softens the Earth."

" My brother is wise. The husband must go without seeing Iraçéma."

The Christian advanced. Poty bid him stop. From the Aljava [1] which Iraçéma had adorned with black and red feathers, and had placed on her husband's shoulders, he selected an arrow.

The Pytiguára drew the bow ; the fleet arrow pierced

---

[1] *Aljava*, Arabic and Portuguese word for quiver.

a Goiamum [1] which was running on the banks of the lake, and stopped only where the feathers would not allow it to enter farther.

The warrior thrust the arrow into the ground with the prey transfixed and turned towards Coatyábo.

"My brother may now set out contentedly. Iraçéma will follow his trail; arriving here, she will see his arrow and obey his will."

Martim smiled; and breaking a branch of the Maracujá—the flower of remembrance—he twined it round the arrow and advanced, followed by Poty.

Soon the two warriors disappeared amongst the trees; the heat of the sun had already dried their footsteps on the banks of the lake. Iraçéma became uneasy, and followed her husband's trail as far as the tableland. Gentle shades already mottled the prairies when she reached the brink of the lake. Her eyes detected the arrow of her husband thrust into the ground, and the pierced Goiamum with the broken branch, and they filled with tears.

"He commands Iraçéma to go backwards like the Goiamum, and to keep his remembrance like the Maracujá, which retains its flower until death."

The daughter of the Tabajáras slowly retraced her steps backwards without turning her body, and never taking her eyes off the arrow of her warrior till she reached the cabin. Here she sat down on the threshold, and bent her forehead on her knees, till sleep soothed the pain in her breast. Hardly had the day broken, when she directed her hasty steps to the lake, and arrived at its bank. The arrow was still there, as it had been the evening before. Then he had not returned.

From this time till the bath hour, instead of seeking the lake of beauty, where hitherto she had bathed with such pleasure, she came to that which had seen

---

[1] *Goiamum*, a large Brazilian crab which courses backwards.

her husband abandon her. She would sit down close to the arrow until night came, and then seek the cabin.

She would set out in early morning, as hurriedly as she would return slowly in the evening. The same warriors who had seen her so joyous in the waters of Porangába now met her sad and alone, like the widowed heron on the river-banks. Hence they called the spot, "of the Mocejana,"[1] or "of the forsaken."

One day when the beautiful daughter of Araken was lamenting on the brink of the Mocejana Lake, a strident voice from the top of a Carnaúba cried out her name—

"Iraçéma! Iraçéma!"

Raising her eyes, she saw amongst the palm-fronds her beautiful Jandáia flapping its wings and ruffling its feathers with the joy of seeing her.

The remembrance of her country, extinguished by love, burned again in her thoughts. She saw the beautiful plains of the Ipú; the sides of the mountain-range where she was born, and the Wigwam of Araken; and she felt Saudades; but even at this moment she did not repent of having abandoned them.

Her voice gushed forth in song. The Jandáia opened its wings, fluttered around, and settled on her shoulder. It stretched its neck and rubbed itself against her throat; it smoothed her hair with its black beak, and pecked her small red lips, as if it mistook them for a Pitanga.[2]

Iraçéma remembered how ungrateful she had been to the Jandáia, forgetting it at the time of her happiness, and now it came to console her in her sorrow.

This evening she did not return alone to the cabin,

---

[1] *Mocejana* is a lake and village two leagues from the capital of Ceará. The word means "what made abandon," "the place of abandoning," and "occasion of abandoning."

[2] A small red fruit in Brazil, the *Pitanga* myrtle berry.

and all next day her agile fingers wove a beautiful cage of straw, which she lined with the soft wool of the Monguba,[1] to receive her companion and friend.

On the following dawn the voice of the Jandáia awoke her. The beautiful bird left its mistress no more, either because it could never weary of seeing her after so long an absence, or because instinct told it that she needed a companion in her sad solitude.

CHAPTER XXVII.

ONE evening Iraçéma saw from afar two warriors advancing on the sea-beach. Her heart beat more quickly.

An instant afterwards, she forgot in the arms of her husband the many days of yearning and desolation which she had passed in the solitary Wigwam.

Again her graces and endearments filled the eyes of the Christian, and gladness once more dwelt in his soul.

Like the dry plain, which, when the thick fog comes, grows green again and is spangled with flowers, so the beautiful daughter of the forest revived at the return of her husband, and her beauty was adorned with soft and tender smiles.

Martim and his brother had arrived at the Taba of Jacaúna as the Inúbia was sounding. They led Poty's thousand bowmen to the combat. Again the Taba-járas, in spite of the alliance with the white Tapuias of the Mearim, were overcome by the brave Pyti-guáras.

Never had such an obstinate fight been fought,

---

[1] *Monguba*, a tree with its fruit full of downy cotton, like that of the Sumaúma, only black, which gives its name to part of the Serra of Maranguape.

nor had so disputed a victory been won on the plains watered by the Acaraú and the Camoçim. The valour was equal on both sides, and neither nation would have been victor, had not the God of War already decided to give these shores to the race of the white warrior allied to the Pytiguáras.

Immediately after triumphing, the Christian returned to the sea-beach where he had built his Wigwam. He felt anew in his soul the thirst of love, and he trembled to think that Iraçéma might have deserted the place which had formerly been peopled by happiness.

The Christian loved the Daughter of the Forest once more, as at first, when it appeared that time could not exhaust his heart. But a few short suns sufficed to wither these flowers of a heart exiled from its country.

The Imbú,[1] son of the mountains, if it spring up in the plains where the wind or the birds have borne its seed, finding good and fresh ground, may perhaps one day dome itself with green foliage and bear flowers. But a single breath of the sea suffices to wither it; the leaves strew the ground, the blossoms are carried away by the breeze.

Like the Imbú on the plains was the heart of the white warrior in the savage land. Friendship and love had accompanied him and sustained him for a time; now, however, far from his home and his people, he felt himself in a desert. The friend and the wife did not suffice any longer to his existence, full of great and noble projects of ambition.

He passed the suns, once so short, now so long, on the beach, listening to the moaning of the wind and the sobbing of the waves. His eyes, lost in the immensity of the horizon, sought, but in vain, to espy

---

[1] *Imbú*, a fruit growing abundantly on the Serra of Araripe, not on the shore; it is savoury, and resembles the Cajá (see note I, page 12).

upon the transparent blue the whiteness of a sail wandering over the seas. At a short distance from the cabin, at the edge of the ocean, was a dune of sand. The fishermen called it Jacarécanga,[1] on account of its resemblance to a crocodile's head. From the bosom of the white sands scorched by the ardent sun flowed a pure fresh water ; thus pain distils sweet tears of relief and consolation. To this hill the Christian would repair, and remain there meditating upon his destiny. Sometimes the idea of returning to his own country and people would cross his mind, but he knew that Iraçéma would accompany him, and this thought gnawed his heart. Each step that took Iraçéma farther from her native plains, now that she no longer could nestle in his heart, was to rob her of a portion of her life.

Poty knows that Martim desires to be alone, and discreetly withdraws. The warrior knows what afflicts his brother's soul, and hopes all things from time, which alone hardens the warrior's heart, like the core of the Jacarandá.

Iraçéma also avoids the eyes of her husband, because she already perceives that those eyes, so much loved, are troubled at her sight, and, instead of filling with delight at her beauty as formerly, now seem to turn wearily away. But *her* eyes never tire of following apart, and at a distance, her Lord and Warrior, who had made them captive.

Woe to her ! . . . The blow had struck home to her heart, and, like the Copaiba,[2] wounded in the core, she shed tears in one continuous stream.

---

[1] *Jacarécanga*, a hill of white sand on the beach at Ceará, famed for a fountain of pure fresh water. The word means "crocodile's head."

[2] *Copaiba*, a sort of sovereign balsam—copayva.

CHAPTER XXVIII.

ONCE the sobs of Iraçéma reached the Christian's soul. His eyes sought her all around, and could not find her.

The daughter of Araken was sitting at some distance upon the turfy grass in the midst of a green clump of Ubaias; weeping veiled her beautiful face, and the teardrops that rolled down her cheeks one after another fell upon her bosom where the offspring of love already breathed and grew. Thus fall the leaves of the flourishing tree before the ripening of its fruit.

"What wrings the tears from the heart of Iraçema?"

"The Cajueiro [1] weeps and is sad when it becomes a dry trunk. Iraçéma lost her happiness when her Lord separated from her."

"Am I not near thee?"

"The *body* of Coatyábo is here, but his soul flies to the Land of his Fathers, and seeks the white virgin who awaits him."

Martim was grieved. The large black eyes that the Indian fixed on him pierced him to the heart's core.

"The White Warrior is *thy* husband; he belongs to *thee*."

The beautiful Tabajára smiled in her sorrow.

"How long is it that he has withdrawn his spirit from Iraçéma? Once his feet guided him to the cool Serras and the glad tablelands; his foot loved to tread the land of happiness and to follow the steps of his wife; now he seeks alone the scorching sands, because the sea which murmurs there comes from the plains where he was born, and the hill of sand, because from its top he can descry the passing Igára."

[1] The tree of the *Cajú*.

" It is his anxiety to fight the Tupinambá whic.ı
guides the warrior's steps to the borders of the sea,"
said the Christian.

Iraçéma continued—

" His lip has dried towards his wife, as the sugar-
cane when the great suns burn ; it then loses its
sweet honey, and the withered leaves play never
more in the wind. Now he only speaks to the sea-
beach breeze, that it may carry back his voice to the
Cabin of his Fathers."

" The voice of the White Warrior is only calling his
brothers to defend the cabin of Iraçéma and the
land of his son when the enemy shall come ! "

The wife shook her head.

" When Coatyábo walks in the plains, his eyes avoid
the fruit of the Genipapo, and seeks the white thorn ;
its fruit is savoury, but it has the colour of the Tabajáras. The thorn bears a white flower, like the cheeks
of the pale virgin. If the birds sing, his ear no longer
cares to listen to the sweet song of the Graúna, but he
opens his soul to the cry of the Japim,[1] because it has
golden feathers like the hair of her whom he loves."

" Sorrow dims the sight of Iraçéma and embitters
her lip. But gladness will soon return to the wife's
soul, as the green leaves bud again on the tree."

" When the White Warrior's son has left the bosom
of Iraçéma she will die, like the Abaty [2] after it has
yielded its fruit. Then he will have nothing to detain
him in a foreign land."

" Thy voice burns, daughter of Araken, like the
winds which blow in the great heat from the deserts
of Ico.[3] Wouldst thou abandon thy husband ? "

" Does the white warrior see that beautiful Jacarandá
which rises to the clouds ? At its feet still lies the

[1] *Japim*, a golden bird with black specks, whose name signifies " to suffer."

[2] *Abaty* means rice.

[3] *Ico*, a south-eastern portion of the province of Ceará.

dry root of the leafy myrtle, which every winter bears
foliage and red berries to embrace and cover its brother
tree. If it did not die, the Jacarandá would not have
sun enough to reach that height. Iraçéma is the Folha
escura [1] which creates darkness in Coatyabo's soul.
She must fall, that gladness may shine within his
breast."

The Christian threw his arms round the waist of the
beautiful Indian and strained her to his heart. His
lips sought hers in a kiss, but it was harsh and bitter.

CHAPTER XXIX.

POTY returned from the bath. He follows the trail
of Coatyábo in the sand, and ascends the height of
Jacarécanga. Here he finds the warrior on the summit, standing upright, with his eyes straining, and his
arms stretched towards the broad seas.

The Pytiguára follows his gaze, and discovers a
large Igára ploughing the green waters and driven on
by the wind.

"It is the great Igára of my brother's Nation sent to
seek him."

The Christian sighed.

"They are the White Warriors, enemies of his race,
who seek, for a war of vengeance, the shores of the
brave Pytiguára nation. They were routed with the
Tabajáras on the banks of the Camoçim. Now they
come with their friends the Tupinambás by the way
of the sea."

"My brother is a Great Chief. What thinks he that
his brother Poty should do?"

[1] *Folha escura*, the myrtle which the Indians call Capixuna or
dark-leaved. Iraçéma used it as a symbol of the ennui she
produced in her husband.

"Summon the Hunters of the Soipé and the Fishers the Trahiry. We will hasten to encounter them."

Poty awoke the voice of the Inubia, and the two warriors set out for Mocoribe.

Soon they saw hastening from all parts the braves of Jaguarassú and Camoropim to respond to the War-cry. The brother of Jacaúna warned them of the enemy's approach.

The great Maracatim [1] flew upon the waters along the coast, which extends as far as the margins of the Parnahyba. [2]

The moon began to increase; when the ship left the waters of the Mearim, contrary winds drove it into the high seas, far beyond its destination.

The Pytiguára warriors, in order not to startle the enemy, hide themselves amongst the Cajueiros, and follow the great Igára along the shore. During the day the white sails are conspicuous, and by night the ship's lights pierced the sea's darkness like fireflies lost in the forest.

Many suns they marched thus. They pass beyond the Camoçim, and at last they tread the beautiful shores of the Bay of Parrots. [3]

Poty sends a warrior to the great Jacaúna and prepares for the combat. Martim, who had mounted the hill of sand, knew that the Maracatim would seek shelter under the lee of the land, and warns his brother.

The sun was already rising. The Guaraciaba [4] warriors and their friends the Tupinambás run along

---

[1] *Maracatim* is a large ship which rises at the prow. Little boats or canoes were called Igára, meaning "lady of the water."

[2] *Parnahyba*, a large river of Piauhy, on the north coast of Brazil.

[3] *Bahia dos papagaios*. It is the Bay of Jericoacoara, and means "Bay of the plain of the parrots," and is one of the best parts of Ceará.

[4] *Guaraciaba* means "yellow-haired." These were the French settlers at Maranhão.

the waves in light Pirogos [1] to make the shore. They form a great arch, like a shoal of fish crossing the current of a river.

In the middle are the fire-warriors, [2] who carry the lightning; on each wing the warriors of Mearim, who brandish the tomahawk. But no nation ever drew the bow so unerringly as the great Pytiguáras, and Poty was the greatest Chief of all the Chiefs who carried the Inubia of war. At his side marches his brother, as great a Chief as himself, and learned in the stratagems of the white race, with hair like the sun.

During the night the Pytiguáras had by his directions fixed into the beach a strong Caiçára, or stockade of thorns, and had raised against it a wall of sand, where the "lightning" might cool and extinguish itself. Here they await the foe. Martim orders other warriors to man the tops of the highest palms, and there, screened by the broad fronds, to make ready for the moment of attack.

The arrow of Poty was the first which left the beach, and the Guaraciába chief was the first hero that bit the dust upon the strange soil.

The thunders roar from the right of the white warriors, but the bolts only burrow themselves in the sand or dive into the sea.

The Pytiguára arrows now fall from the heavens, then they fly from the earth and bury themselves in the enemies' hearts. Each warrior falls riddled with many arrows, like the prey for which the Piranhas [3] fight in the waters of the lake.

The enemy once more embark in the canoes, and return to the Maracatim to fetch bigger and heavier thunders, which neither one man nor two could manage.

---

[1] *Pirogos*, canoes.
[2] *Guerreiros do fogo*—the French, from their guns.
[3] *Piranha*, a fresh-water fish, a ferocious kind of salmon. It lives in lakes and dead waters, and has teeth which bite like scissors.

When they were returning, the Chief of the Fishers, who swims in the sea-waters like the agile Camoropim, from whom he took his name, casts himself into the waves and dives. Before the foam had passed away from the place where he disappeared, the enemy's canoe had sunk as if it had been swallowed by a whale.

The night came and brought with it repose.

At dawn of day, the Maracatim was flying in the horizon towards the banks of the Mearim. Jacaúna arrived, not in time for the fight, but for the feast of victory.

At the same hour that the songs of the Pytiguára warriors were celebrating the conquest of the Guaraciábas, the first son born to this Land of Liberty begotten by the blood of the white race, saw the light in the plains of Porangába.

CHAPTER XXX.

IRAÇÉMA thought that her bosom would burst. She sought the banks of the river where grows the Coqueiro-palm, and clasped the trunk of the tree till a tiny cry inundated her whole being with joy.

The young mother, proud of so much happiness, took the tender one in her arms, and with him cast herself into the limpid waters of the river. Then she gave him the delicate breast, and her eyes devoured him with sorrow and love.

"Thou art Moacyr,[1] the fruit of my anguish."

The Jandáia perched at the top of the palm tree repeated "Moacyr;" and from that time the friendly bird united in its song the names of both mother and son.

[1] *Moacyr* or "son of suffering," from *moacy*, pain, and *ira*, a desinence meaning "that comes from."

The innocent slept ; Iraçéma sighed.

" The Jaty makes honey in the sweet-smelling trunk of the Sassafrax ;[1] during the month of flowers it flies from branch to branch collecting the juice to fill the comb, but it does not taste its sweetness's reward, because the Irára[2] devours in one night the whole swarm. Thy mother, also, child of my sorrow, will never taste the joy of seeing the smile on thy lips."

The young mother fastened over her shoulders a broad swathe[3] of soft cotton, which she had made to carry her child always fastened upon her hip. She then followed over the sands the trail of her spouse, who had been gone three suns. She walked gently, not to awake the little one, that slept like a bird under the maternal wing.

When she arrived at the great hill of sand, she saw that the trail of Martim and Poty continued along the beach, and guessed that they were gone to the war. Her heart sighed, but her eyes sought the face of her babe.

She turned her face back towards the Mocoribe.

" Thou art the Hill of Gladness, but for Iraçéma thou bringest nothing but sorrow."

Returning, the mother placed the still - sleeping child in his father's hammock, widowed and solitary, in the cabin centre. She lay down upon the mat where she had slept since the time her husband's arms had ceased opening to receive her.

The morning light entered the cabin. Iraçéma saw the shade of a warrior come in with it.

Cauby was standing in the doorway.

---

[1] *Sassafrax*, a well-known tree, growing both in North and South America, much used in medicine.

[2] *Irára*, a kind of bush-dog, which attacks beehives and devours the honey.

[3] *Faxa*, vulgarly called *Typoia;* swathing or swaddling clothes.

The wife of Martim sprang up with one bound to protect her child. Her brother raised his sad eyes from the hammock to her face, and spoke with a still sadder voice.

"It was not vengeance which drew the warrior Cauby to the plains of the Tabajáras ; he has already forgiven. It was a longing to see Iraçéma, who took away with her all his gladness."

"Then welcome be the warrior Cauby to the cabin of his brother," said the wife, embracing him.

"The fruit of thy bosom sleeps in this hammock, and the eyes of Cauby long to behold it."

Iraçéma opened the fringe of feathers and showed the babe's fair face. Cauby contemplated it for some time, and then laughing said—

"He has sucked the soul of my sister,"[1] and he kissed in the mother's eyes the image of the child, fearing lest his touch might hurt it.

The trembling voice of the girl cried—

"Does Araken still live upon the earth ?"

"Hardly ; since my sister left him his head bent upon his bosom, and it rose up no more."

"Tell him that Iraçéma is already dead, that he may be consoled."

Cauby's sister prepared food for the warrior, and slung in the porch the hammock of hospitality, that he might repose after the fatigues of the journey. When the traveller was refreshed, he arose with these words—

"Say, where is Iraçéma's husband and Cauby's brother, that the braves may exchange the embrace of friendship ?"

The sighing lips of the unhappy wife moved like the petals of the cactus-flower stirred by a breeze,

---

[1] *Chupou tua alma.* A child in Tupy is called *Pitanga*, from *piter*, to suck, and *anga*, soul—suck-soul. Cauby meant that it resembled the mother, and had absorbed a portion of her spirit.

and remained speechless. But tears rolled from her eyes in big drops.

Cauby's face clouded.

" Iraçéma's brother thought that sadness remained in the plains she had abandoned, because she took with her all the smiles of those who loved her ! "

Iraçéma dried her eyes.

" The husband of Iraçéma has left with the warrior Poty for the shores of the Acaraú. Before three suns shall have illuminated the earth he will return, and with him gladness to the soul of the wife."

" The warrior Cauby awaits him, to know what he has done with the smile which lived on Iraçéma's lips."

The voice of the Tabajára grew hoarse, and his restless step walked at random up and down the cabin.

CHAPTER XXXI.

SOFTLY sang Iraçéma, rocking the hammock to soothe her son.

The beach sands cracked beneath the strong firm foot of the Tabajára brave, who came from the sea-border with an abundance of fish.

The young mother crossed the fringes of the hammock that the flies might not tease her sleeping babe, and went forth to meet her brother.

" Cauby will return to the mountains of the Tabajáras ! " she said gently.

The warrior's brow clouded over.

" Iraçéma sends away her brother from her Wigwam that he may not see the sorrow which fills it."

" Araken had many sons in his youth. Some were carried off by war, and they died like braves ; others

chose wives, and begot in their turn numerous offspring.   Araken had but two children of his old age.
Iraçéma is for him like the dove which the hunter
has stolen from its nest.   Alone remains with the old
Pagé the warrior Cauby, to sustain his bent frame and
to guide his tremulous steps."

"Cauby will depart when the shade shall leave the
face of Iraçéma.   As lives the night-star, so lives Iraçéma in her sorrow.   Only the eyes of her husband
can banish the darkness from her brow.   Go, in
order that his sight may not wax dim at the sight of
Cauby !"

"Iraçéma's brother will depart to please her, but
he will return every time the Cajueiro flowers to feel
in his heart the child of her bosom."

He entered the cabin.   Iraçéma took the child
from the hammock, and both mother and son remained pressed to the heart of Cauby.   He then
passed through the door, and soon disappeared amid
the trees.

Iraçéma, dragging along her trembling steps, accompanied him for some distance, till he was lost to
sight on the skirts of the forest.   Then she stopped ;
when the cry of the Jandáia, accompanied by the
infant's wail, recalled her to the cabin ; only the cold
sand upon which she had sat, kept the secret of the
tears which it had drank.

The young mother gave her child the breast, but
the babe's moan was not hushed.   The scanty milk
refused to flow.

The blood of the unhappy girl had been thinned
by the ever-flowing tears of which her eyes had not
wearied, and none came to her bosom, where the first
nourishment of life is formed.

She dissolved the white Cariman [1] and prepared

---

[1] *Cariman*, strained mandioca—a porridge of mandioca ; from
caric, to run, and *mani*, manioc.

over the fire the Mingáo [1] to nourish her son. When the sun gilded the mountain-crests she set out towards the forest, carrying on her bosom the sleeping child.

In the thickness of the wood was found the lair of the absent Irára; the pups, still small, were whining and rolling over one another. The beautiful Tabajára crept softly up to it. She made for her child a cradle of a soft bough of the Maracujá, and sat down near it.

She took one by one into her lap all the pups of the Irára, and abandoned to their famished mouths her bosom, beautiful as the red Pitanga, which she had anointed with the honey of the bee. The hungry young ones fastened upon it, and greedily drained her breasts.

Iraçéma felt pain hitherto unknown to her; they seemed to exhaust her life. At last, however, her bosom began to swell, and the milk, still tinged with the life-fluid of which it is formed, gushed forth.

The happy mother cast away the little Iráras, and, full of joy, appeased the hunger of the babe. He is now doubly Moacyr, the son of pain, once born of Iraçema, and secondly nourished by her.

The daughter of Araken at last began to feel that her veins were drying up, and withal her life, embittered by sorrow, rejected the nourishment which might have restored her strength. Tears and sighs had alike banished the smile and the appetite from her beautiful mouth.

---

[1] *Mingáo*, a sort of porridge of which the Brazilians are very fond; it is made of mandioca-flour, sugar, eggs, cinnamon, &c., &c.

CHAPTER XXXII.

The sun declines. Japy springs out of the forest and runs towards the Wigwam-door.

Iraçéma, sitting with her child upon her bosom, basks in the sun's ray, for she feels the cold shivering through her frame. On seeing the faithful messenger of her husband, hope revived in her heart. She would have arisen to meet her Lord and Warrior, but her weak limbs refused to obey her will.

She fell helpless against a Wigwam-prop.

Japy licked the inanimate hand, and jumped playfully, to make the child laugh, with little barks of joy. At times it rushed to the forest skirts and barked to call its master, and then it ran back to the cabin to fondle the mother and the child.

At this time Martim was treading the yellow prairies of Tauapé;[1] his inseparable brother, Poty, marched by his side.

Eight moons[2] had sped since he had left the beach of Jacarécanga. After conquering the Guaraciábas in the Bay of the Parrots, the Christian warrior left for the banks of the Mearim, where lived the savage allies of the Tupinambás.

Poty and his warriors accompanied him. After they had crossed the flowing arm of the sea which comes from the Serra of Tauatinga[3] and bathes the plains where men fish for Piau,[4] they finally saw the

---

[1] *Tauapé* means "place of yellow clay." It is on the road to Maranguape.

[2] *Moons* are months, as suns are days.

[3] *Tauatinga*, a Serra in the province of Piauhy where rises the Parahyba river.

[4] *Piau*, a fish which gives its name to the river and province of Piauhy.

beaches of the Mearim, and the Velha Taba [1] of the barbarous Tapuia.

The race of the Sunny-hair gained more and more the friendship of the Tupinambás, the number of the white warriors increased, and they had already raised in the island the great Itaoca [2] to send forth their lightning.

When Martim had seen what was wanted, he retraced his way to the prairies of the Porangába, which he now treads. Already he hears the hoarse grating of the tide on the beach of the Mocoribe ; already the breath of the ocean wave fans his cheek.

The nearer his step approaches the Wigwam, the slower and more heavy it becomes. He dreads to arrive ; he feels that his soul is about to suffer, when the sad heart-weary eyes of his wife shall pierce it.

Long ago had speech deserted his parched lip ; the friend respects this silence, which he well understands. It is the stillness of the waters running over the dark deep places.

As soon as the two warriors reached the river-banks, they heard the barking of the dog calling them and the cry of the Jandáia in lamentation.

They were now very near the Wigwam, which was hid only by a slip of forest. The Christian stopped, pressing his hand to his bosom to still his heart, which beat like the Poraquî. [3]

" The bark of Japy is of gladness," quoth the chief.

" Because he has arrived ; but the voice of the Jandáia is of sadness. Will the absent warrior find peace in the bosom of the deserted wife, or will Saudades have killed the fruit of her love ? "

The Christian moved forward his dilatory step.

---

[1] *Velha Taba* is the Portuguese of Tapui-tapera, and was the name of one of the Tupinambá settlements in Maranhão.

[2] *Itaoca*, house of stone—fortress.

[3] *Poraquî*, electric fish which jumps ; of flat, broad, and ugly shape.

Suddenly, between the branches of the trees, his eyes beheld sitting at the Wigwam-door Iraçéma with her boy in her lap, and the dog playing about them. His heart carried him there with a bound, and his whole soul rushed to his lips—

"Iraçéma !"

The broken-hearted wife and mother could only open her eyes on hearing the beloved voice. Only with a great effort she can raise the babe in her arms and present it to the father, who gazes at it with ecstatic love.

"Receive the son of thy blood. Thou hast arrived in time ; already my breasts have no nourishment for him."

Placing the child in the paternal arms, the unhappy mother fainted away, like the Jetyca [1] with its uprooted bulb. The husband then saw how pain and sorrow had withered her form ; but beauty still dwelt there, like perfume in the fallen flower of the Manacá. [2]

Iraçéma rose no more from the hammock where the afflicted arms of Martim had placed her. The husband, whose love was born anew with paternal joy, surrounded her with caresses, which filled her soul with its former happiness. But they could not bring her back to life. The stamen of her flower was broken for ever.

"Let the body of thy wife sleep at the foot of the palm-tree which thou lovedst. When the breeze of the sea shall sigh amongst its leaves, Iraçéma will think it is *thy* voice whispering through her hair."

Her lip became silent for ever ; the last spark faded away from the darkening eyes.

Poty supported his brother in his great sorrow. Martim felt how precious in misfortune is a true

---

[1] *Jetyca*, a tree which gives gum.
[2] *Manacá*, a flower well known in Pará. They also call by this name the most beautiful girl in a tribe, or anything of pleasure connected with a feast.

friend; he is like the hill which shelters from the hurricane [1] the trunk of the strong hardy Ubiratan, pierced by the Copim. [2]

The Camoçim received the corpse of Iraçéma, which, steeped in aromatic spices and sweet herbs, was buried at the foot of the palm tree on the river-banks. Martim broke a branch of myrtle, the leaf of sadness, and laid it on the last resting-place of his wife.

The Jandáia, perched at the top of the palm tree, sadly repeated—

" Iraçéma ! "

From that time the Pytiguára warriors who passed by the deserted Wigwam, and who heard the plaintive voice of the devoted bird incessantly calling for its mistress, withdrew with their souls full of sadness from the palm-tree where sang the Jandáia.

And thus it happened that one day, the river where the palm-tree grew, and the prairies through which the river winds, came to be called Ceará. [3]

CHAPTER XXXIII.

THE Cajueiro flowered four times since Martim had left the shores of Ceará, bearing with him in the fragile bark his little son and the faithful dog. The Jandáia would not leave the land where rested its friend and mistress.

[1] In the original *Vendaval*, which is the wind that brings ships home from the West Indies. It is not constant, as the trade-wind, yet it generally ranges between the south and north-west.

[2] *Copim*, a white ant, composed of *co*, a hole, and *pim*, a sting.

[3] *Ceará* is composed of *cemo*, to sing loud, and *ará*, a parroqueet. The above is the legend which gave the province its name.

The first Cearense, still in his cradle, thus became an Emigrant from his Fatherland. Did this announce the destinies of the race to be?

Poty with his warriors awaited on the river-banks. The Christian had promised to return; every morning he climbed the sand-hill and strained his eyes, hoping for a friendly sail to whiten the sea-horizon.

Martim at last returned to the land which had once seen his happiness, and which now sees his bitter regret. When his foot pressed the hot white sand, there spread through his frame a fire which burned his heart: it was the fire of consuming memory.

The flame was extinguished only when he stood on the place where his wife slept, because at that moment his heart overflowed like the trunk of the Jetahy[1] in the great heats, and refreshed his grief with a shower of tears.

Many warriors of his race accompanied the white Chief to found with him the Christian Mayri. There came also a Priest of his Faith, black-robed, to plant the Cross upon this savage soil.

Poty was the first who knelt at the foot of the Sacred Wood. He would not allow anything again to part himself and his white brother; for this reason, as they had but one heart, he wished that both might have the same God.

He received in baptism the name of the Saint[2] whose day it was, and of the King he was about to serve; besides these two, his own translated into the tongue of his new brethren.

His fame increased, and it is still the pride of the land in which he first saw the light.

The Mayri which Martim founded on the river-banks within the shores of Ceará flourished. The word of the true God budded in the savage land, and

---

[1] *Jetahy,* a kind of Hymenæa from which a yellow gum exudes.

[2] Antonio Phelipe Camarão.

the holy Church-bells re-echoed through the valleys where once bellowed the Maracá.

Jacaúna came to inhabit the plains of the Porangába, to be near his white friend. Camerão (Poty) placed the Taba of his warriors on the banks of the Mocejána. Later, when Albuquerque,[1] the Great Chief of the White Warriors, arrived, Martim and Camarão made for the banks of the Mearim, to chastise the ferocious Tupinambá and to expel the white Tapuia.

The husband of Iraçéma never could behold without the deepest emotion the shores where he had been so happy, and the green leaves under whose shade slept the beautiful Tabajára girl.

Often he would go and sit upon these soft sands, to meditate, and to soothe the bitter Saudade in his heart.

The Jandáias still sang upon the crests of the palm-tree, but no more remembered the sweet name of Iraçema.

On *this* Earth all things pass away!

[1] Jeronimo de Albuquerque, Chief of the Expedition to Maranhão in 1612.

FINIS.

www.ingramcontent.com/pod-product-compliance
Lightning Source LLC
Chambersburg PA
CBHW032146010726
47493CB00008BA/2602